Hunt For The Raven's Spire

The Fae Age, Book Two

E.J. Graham

Winnipeg, Canada

Editors: Alison Cybe & Francisco Feliciano

Published November 2023 by Deep Hearts YA, an imprint of Deep Desires Press and Story Perfect Inc.

Deep Hearts YA
PO Box 51053 Tyndall Park
Winnipeg, Manitoba R2X 3B0
Canada

Visit deepheartsya.com for more great reads.

Dramatis Personae

Clint's Group

Clint, Crystal and Mickey – Half-human, half-fairy teenagers who discovered their heritage during the war with Feth'rael. Crystal is the child of fae death god Feth'rael.

Niana – Princess of Hope's Reach, Clint's fiancée.

Nara – Cornish Pixie, Crystal's romantic partner.

Selina – Non-binary fae child of the US president, Mickey's partner and historical expert of the group.

Marek – Half-Sidhe, half-fae child of uncertain parentage. Although younger than the rest of the group he is one of the most outspoken.

Other Fae

Naarin – Prince of Hope's Reach, commander of the city's military when action needs to be taken.

Nikkela – Naarin's partner, the chief healer of Hope's Reach and one of the city's best archers. Clint's cousin on his mother's side.

Narina – Queen of Hope's Reach, engaged to Clint's uncle, sister to both Naarin and Niana, recently recovered from the strain of having to shield her city almost single-handedly.

Desh'ayi – Nikkela's mother, Clint's aunt, fled Hope's Reach after an attack that killed her husband. Only recently reunited with her daughter.

Human Allies

Rick – Scott's uncle, fiancée of Narina, appointed the UK's ambassador to the fae world after the war with Feth'rael. Acts as much as Narina's emotional rock in times of stress as her partner.

Scott – UK Prime Minister, close friend to Rick, one of the first world leaders to aid the allied forces.

Terry – The US President, father to Selina, survivor of an assassination attempt during the war and fierce defender of his daughter's right.

Izzy – Talented journalist, goddaughter to Terry, who played a major role in exposing Feth'rael's plan to the world.

To Kate, the first person to review Fairy War.
A beautiful human being taken from the world far too soon

Hunt For The Raven's Spire

Chapter 1

Birdsong.

I had been living with the fairies for almost a year and waking up to the sound of unsullied nature still caught me offguard every once in a while. However, it was only when I turned over in the bed and realized Niana had already left it that I remembered what was happening today.

I got up, slipping slightly uneasily into the set of formal clothes one of the fairy tailors had created for me, and took a moment to look in the mirror. It was a dark brown jacket, something I had rarely worn before in my life, with grey trousers and a pair of formal but comfortable shoes, my wings just visible behind my back, shimmering slightly in the light of the room. I walked over to the room's lone window, opening it and looking out upon the city below. Nareena had felt the name of Shadowglen no longer appropriate for a city meant to represent the new world we found ourselves in, and thus it was now called Hope's Reach. Fresh buildings sprawled out in all directions, and fairies could be seen milling around, as decorations were hung through the streets.

"We don't have long to prepare before the guests arrive," came Naarin's unmistakable voice from somewhere below me, causing me to let out a chuckle. Although I couldn't see him from where I stood, I could imagine him being as regimented as he was with the soldiers.

I took a look in the mirror before walking out of the bedroom door. As I walked towards the entrance of the tower, I found myself once again feeling a little uncomfortable at the few soldiers within the palace saluting me as I passed. My relationship with Niana felt fairly ordinary, so being treated like a royal still seemed bizarre. I finally reached the entrance, opening the double doors to find the central square packed with fairies milling around, although the two figures I was looking for stood out from the crowd easily. Queen Nareena, her skin glowing as if it was reflecting the sunlight and dressed in a flowing red dress, was stood talking to an older female fairy. My uncle Rick, who was stood next to her looking more comfortable in a tuxedo than I had seen him a very long time, wasn't holding his fiancee's hand at that moment, but was near enough that she could see she had his support. He smiled as he saw me approaching.

"Where are Mickey and Crystal?" I asked. "I thought they weren't going to miss this commemoration for anything?"

"Crystal and Nara are making sure the banquet hall is presentable," Rick replied, pulling me into a quick hug, Nareena offering me one of her warmest smiles as she noticed me. "Crystal seems to be enjoying indulging her creative side. As for Mickey and Selina, last I heard they were exploring an old fairy archive near Madrid, but they sent a message last night to say they would be back in time for some of today. Looks like someone's been looking for you," he said, indicating somewhere behind me.

I turned to find Niana, dressed in a long blue gown which seemed to have gems like stars stitched into its fabric, walking towards me, pulling me into a delicate kiss.

"Good to see my love polishes up even better than I expected," she said, taking my hand in hers. "It's weird to think this time twelve months ago we were fighting to save the world, I'm glad that's not an annual experience."

At that moment there was a gasp from some of the fairies around us, causing us to turn around in time to see the dignitaries arriving, the Prime Minister and his wife at the front. Selina's father Terry wasn't far behind, followed by the head of the UN who gave me a familiar smile, along with other dignitaries I did not recognise. What caught my eye however was a young woman with two small children, and the wheelchair bound teenage girl who was staying close to her.

"Glad to see your new job is having such a positive effect on you," Scott said, giving my uncle a firm hug, before bending down to kiss Nareena's hand. "I'm glad I came here under better circumstances than we first met your highness. This is King William, the King of the United Kingdom," he said, moving aside to allow Nareena to greet a tall man in a well-pressed suit, the only sign he was a royal was the small crown perched on the top of his head. Although I was curious to watch this meeting, I suddenly felt a hand on my shoulder, turning to find Selina's father stood behind me, offering a handshake.

"I feel like I should apologise for not congratulating you on your engagement sooner," the President said with a wry laugh. "I feel like even Izzy spends more time here than I do," he said, nodding to the young woman I had first met as a journalist, now employed as his press secretary. She was deep in conversation with a male fairy who was even taller than my uncle. He wore plain armour, a brown cloak thrown over his shoulders, a mess of black hair looking as if it had been placed haphazardly on the top of his head. "Are she and Maethra ever going to become a couple?"

"They'll probably get there eventually," Niana replied. "But I know Maethra well enough to know he won't rush anything, he had to be persuaded to become head of the city guard after the end of the war."

"I think it's time for the ceremony to begin," Naarin said, walking over to us. "You guys had better take your seats, I'll show you where to go."

Niana grabbed my hand before we walked away. "Are you sure you're okay?"

I let out a nervous laugh. "Yeah, just…I never quite learned how to deal with interacting with celebrities, it's going to take me time to get used to this. I'll be fine with you here though."

I found myself in the front row of the seats that encircled the large object in the central courtyard, a sheet thrown over it to disguise what it was, while Niana sat to one side of me,

Izzy with her notepad perched on her knees to the other. The young woman and the children I had noticed before were sat in the front row a few seats away from me, the mum occasionally having to chide her children to not run after the sparkly lights dancing in the air. To one side of the hidden object, I could just glimpse Rick and Nareena deep in conversation, unable to decipher anything from that distance, but it didn't take long before the queen walked to the centre of the circle of chairs, letting out a cough to make sure that she had the undivided attention of her audience.

"Ladies and gentlemen, welcome," she said, her voice seeming simultaneously quiet and composed, while also loud enough it would be heard for miles around. "Some of you I have met before, to those I have not, welcome to our great city of Hope's Reach. This is a moment that some of my more recent ancestors feared would never come about again, but we should not forget how this newfound friendship came about. A year ago, our two races came dangerously close to our doom, and while we have much to celebrate it is important we do not forget what it cost us to get here."

She took a moment to turn away, which from where I sat looked as if she was wiping a tear away, before turning back to face us again.

"When I spoke to the US President and the head of the UN in the aftermath we made a decision," she continued. "In order to acknowledge that both our races worked together to save our world we decided we would have memorials in important locations for both of us. Stood outside the UN in New York is a statue to Nightshade…"

Once again, she had to pause, waving Rick's offer of assistance away. "He is…was one of the bravest fairies I ever knew, and it was his last action in this world which ended our enemy's ritual once and for all. I wished to have a human remembered in this city, and I could think of only one."

At a single gesture from her Rick pulled a rope, revealing the statue. It was of Colonel Jack Samson, the young soldier we had met only briefly in New York, the statue so well sculpted it was almost as if he was stood in front of the entire audience.

"I only met Jack once," Nareena said. "But for those fortunate enough to know him, one thing was clear: he had the kind of bravery and selflessness there should be more of in this world. He was a man his widow and children should feel nothing but pride for having known."

It was when the crowd looked at them that I realized who the woman and two children I had noticed among the visitors were, and then I remembered the story of the girl he had died saving, and suddenly the disabled young girl's presence made sense.

"I suspect however that both Nightshade and Jack would not wish us to feel sad for long," Nareena said, finally smiling again. "Our meal will be ready soon, feel free to mingle while we wait."

Niana, Izzy, Rick and I all made a beeline for the platform. Nareena gratefully accepted Rick offering her a hug and a kiss on the forehead as we reached her.

"I told you, you would be fine," Rick said, smiling at Nareena. "If you can face down a lord of the underworld without fear then public speaking is vastly less intimidating experience surely?"

"Thank you for reminding me why I love you," Nareena said, laughing softly. There was a sudden noise from behind her, and we all turned to see the soldier's widow, her two small children, and the young woman he had rescued waiting expectantly. "Katerina, I am glad you could come today."

"Your highness," Katerina said, trying to curtsey while keeping hold of the little girl and boy's hands. "I don't know how to repay you for that speech, you—"

"Katerina, you do not need to repay me," Nareena said, curtseying herself. "Besides, do not call me your highness, you have the right to call me Nareena." The two shared a warm hug before the Queen knelt down in front of the two children. "So you must be Jake and Rosie, it is a—" She was caught off-guard by the fact both children suddenly hugged her tightly, causing Nareena to let out an almost childlike laugh herself.

"Darlings, don't just throw yourselves at the poor lady," Katerina said, unable to stifle her own laughter.

"I don't mind," Nareena said as they finally let go. "I have long believed we can all learn much from our children." She turned to the other young woman. "How are you holding up Nicole? I've kept an eye on your progress, you have a bright future ahead of you I believe."

"I haven't done anything remarkable," Nicole said, blushing slightly at the sudden attention she had garnered. "Most people in my school don't even know who I am."

"You don't have to be famous to achieve something,"

Nareena said, kneeling in front of her. "It's not who you are that makes an impact on this world, it is what you do with your life which does." From where I was stood, I could see her brush a tear from her face, but before she could say anything else the sound of a loud bell cut through the still air around us, causing both human and fairy alike to look around. "Naarin, is that—"

"The Bell of the Sentinels," Naarin said, taking a step towards the gates to the city.

"The bell of what?" I asked, looking between the two siblings.

"The Bell of the Sentinels," Niana replied. "The Sentinels who guard the borders of our city cannot ordinarily enter in their military garb, that way if they have to come here armed, we know something serious has occurred. Brother, what shall we do?"

"Nareena, remain here with the delegates," Naarin said to the Queen. "Clint, Niana, come with me."

Before we had a chance to ask further questions, he launched himself into the air, Niana and I having to fly as fast as we could manage but eventually we caught up with him. It only took a few moments to see what had caused the bell to be rung: hurrying up the central street towards where the dignitaries were came two figures in long green cloaks, one carrying the prone form of a young woman in a plain blue t-shirt and jeans, with unkempt brown hair; the other's cargo to even my relatively inexperienced eye was an extremely young fairy, its barely formed wings folded against its back. Just as one appeared about to stumble

Naarin managed to land, taking the unconscious girl from him, Niana landing just after.

"What happened?" Naarin asked as he looked at the girl.

"We found them near the entrance to the old tunnels," the Sentinel replied between deep breaths. "We are not sure how they got there, but the girl…" he didn't finish the sentence, simply lifted her shirt far enough we could all see a nasty cut across her stomach which had turned a deep purple colour.

"Shall I get Nikkela?" Niana asked.

"We don't have time," Naarin replied. "Clint, are you sure you're up to this?"

"I can try," I replied. I knelt down next to Naarin, reaching out my right hand towards the wound. But as I attempted to touch it I felt a sudden, inexplicable jolt of pain through my hand, at the same moment seeing a sudden dark blur appear momentarily in front of my eyes before vanishing as quickly as it had appeared.

"Are you okay Clint?" Naarin asked, giving me a confused look.

"Yeah…Yeah, I'm fine," I answered, trying to regain my composure, before moving my hand towards the wound again, feeling confident when there was not a similar reaction as before. However, the minute my hand touched the wound, the pain came back even worse than before, and the blur became far clearer. I could see was a darkness only interrupted by a pair of yellow eyes with no pupils, which seemed to be looking straight into my very soul. There was a sense of an entity but it's body was entirely transparent

I wasn't sure how long I had been like this, but I suddenly found myself looking up into Niana's concerned face. "I...I can't heal her," I stammered. "Whatever hurt her...this is dark magic, something I've never felt before now. I...I don't even know how that's possible."

"Stay with us," Naarin was saying to the girl as I sat up, realizing I had collapsed exactly where I had been kneeling when I attempted to heal her. The girl was now conscious, but her eyes were barely open and despite her lips moving no sound seemed to be forthcoming. "Can you tell me your name?"

"Drak..." the girl managed to get out. "Show them..." she said, placing something in Naarin's hand, before a final rattling breath escaped her, her body going still as Nikkela landed in front of Naarin. In a moment that reminded me of the time after the battle of the Glade that had shown me the love shared between the two, Nikkela pulled Naarin into a hug, no words passing between them.

"Prince Naarin," one of the Sentinels said after a few moments. "The girl, what was it she gave to you?"

"What do you..." Naarin started asking, before he remembered what the fairy meant. I couldn't see what he was looking at, but I could see the colour suddenly drain from his face.

"What is it Naarin?" Nikkela asked. "What's going on?"

"Nikkela, find my sister," Naarin replied. "Tell her our guests need to be taken inside now, and then she, Rick, Scott and Terry had better meet us in the Grand Hall." He turned to me and Niana as Nikkela took off again. "Find Crystal and Nara, they'd better join us too."

"What is it brother?" Niana asked as he turned away from us. "What did she give you?"

"If it's what I believe, something bad," the Prince replied. "Something bad for everyone."

Elsewhere in the world, a raven wound its way through a mountain range was winding through a mountain range, its destination visible for miles around: a castle set on a lower slope of one of the larger peaks, but whose tower stretched above almost all its surroundings. The bird didn't stop until it reached a window near the top of the tower, landing on its sill and knocking its beak against the wooden shutters drawn across it. For a few moments nothing seemed to happen, but then the shutters suddenly opened inwards, revealing a room barely illuminated by the light now pouring into the room. While there was a pool of light in the centre of the room only the outline of an occasional shelf could be seen beyond. After a few moments the bird leapt off the windowsill, but by the time it landed in the room it had changed; in place of a bird was a small but fearsome looking fairy, long black robes stretching covering most of his body, a wickedly sharp blade strapped over his back. He knelt down, waiting for some kind of signal.

"Did you ensure they got the message?" came a voice from somewhere in the darkness, the fairy nodding silently in response. "Good, I had expected this to be far more difficult. I do so enjoy pleasant surprises. You had best return to them, ensure that we are not discovered *too* quickly."

As the voice finished its sentence the fairy jumped into the air, by the time it had returned to the windowsill it had returned to its raven form, turning back in time to catch a glimpse of a cloak that seemed composed of features as dark as his own, moving in the darkness beyond as it heard the last words before it departed.

"After all, the Lord of Ravens needs time to prepare, we're about to have some very…entertaining guests."

Chapter 2

Niana, Naarin and I sat in sombre silence in the meeting hall as we waited, the quiet only broken by the doors opening as Nareena, my uncle, Izzy and the two leaders walked in, taking the remaining seats around the table before the Queen cleared her throat.

"I am sure by now we are all aware a tragedy occurred here today," Nareena said, not making eye contact with any of us. "Naarin, can you explain exactly what has happened?"

"Approximately three quarters of an hour ago a young woman of no more than twenty was discovered outside the walls of this city," Naarin replied. "Unfortunately, despite our best efforts," at that moment he gave me a sympathetic smile before continuing, "her injuries were too severe." He allowed a few moments for the news to sink in among all those around the table. For a moment I thought I could hear Niana saying a prayer under her breath.

"What of the cargo she brought with her?" I asked when it became clear no-one else would break the silence. "The baby? Whatever it was she handed to you?"

"The baby is a mystery," Naarin said, rolling up his

sleeve to reveal what looked like a tattoo in the shape of a single red rose on his wrist. "We haven't told you children this because up to this point it has not seemed necessary to do so, but we do not have baptism as you humans would understand. However, shortly after birth, fairies are marked with a…tattoo that represents their home city, this is the one for this city."

"And the child?" Niana asked.

"Bears a tattoo that matches none of our records," Naarin replied. "I would not claim to know every fairy city on Earth, but this one is…different. We will have to explore further unless we hear about any missing fairy children. And then," he said, reaching into his coat and pulling out a small piece of parchment. "There is the reason I called this meeting originally: before she died the girl passed me information that should concern us all."

As he passed it to Niana, and the piece of paper slowly worked its way around the table, I couldn't help being fascinated by the different responses its contents elicited from the readers: human readers seemed puzzled by its contents, whereas Niana and Nareena had looks which ranged from shock to sheer horror. Finally, Niana passed it to me, and I read it with a mix of anticipation and concern.

"The gates of the Ravenspire have opened, all comers are welcome to see its secrets," read the small note scrawled on the paper.

"I hate to sound ignorant," I said, handing it back to Naarin. "But what exactly *is* the Ravenspire?"

"There are all sorts of legends about the place," Niana replied. "Most of which modern fairies assume are exaggerated legends. I'm not sure any of the stories are actually true."

"I might be able to help you with that," came a voice from behind me, causing us all to turn around in time to find Selina and Mickey had entered the room. Selina was dressed in a plain black top and short skirt, a large, dusty looking book tucked under their arm. Mickey on the other hand was in a red t-shirt and shorts, a pair of sandals on his feet indicating that they had not stopped to change out of their vacation clothes before coming into the room. Terry drew Selina into a warm embrace, which Selina returned after a few moments, before he shared a similar embrace with Mickey. Selina walked over, placing the book on the table. "Luckily for you all I managed to retrieve this book from *La Biblioteca de la Magia de las Hadas* in Madrid," she said, stifling a laugh at the concern on her father's face. "I didn't steal it, when I told the librarian about the notes that were circulating, it was he who suggested I bring this book with me."

"Are you saying this message has been passed to other people?" Naarin asked, the colour seeming to have drained from his face, much as it had when he first read the note.

"I'm not sure how many copies of this note exist," Selina replied. "One thing I know for certain is that Naarin's concern is well founded." She opened the book, and seemed to be humming an unfamiliar tune as she flicked through it, eventually exclaiming as she reached a page that caused her to turn the book to face everyone. On one page was nothing but a wall of text, but on the other was a drawing of an immense tower, at the base of which huddled a group of small buildings, the background seemed dominated by large mountain peaks. "To some people the Ravenspire is the fairy equivalent of Atlantis, a place many claim is awaiting rediscovery, while others claim is nothing but a myth created by those unable to understand events taking place around them."

"If this note is genuine," Rick said, stroking his chin thoughtfully, "then I suspect the Ravenspire has more of a grounding in fact than the Atlanteans ever did."

"The Ravenspire is real," Selina replied. "I assume you all know this is far from the first time that humans and fairies have co-existed? There was a time when human and fairy society was almost impossible to tell apart, and during that time there lived a human whose name has been lost to memory. He was a trickster, he claimed to be able to turn any metal into gold, but of course he was a liar. It went the same way every time, his lies were discovered and he was chased out of the town. He was on the verge of destitution when he crossed paths with a fairy called Maraile."

At the mention of that name a gasp rippled through the fairies: Crystal and I shared a confused look.

"Who is Maraile?" Mickey asked. "I feel like I've heard that name before, but I don't know where from."

"Maraile is a story told to young fairies to frighten them," Nareena replied, trying to regain her composure. "A story of the dangers of unleashing dark magic. At least, that was what I believed it was, I take it I have been misinformed?"

"Maraile was real," Selina replied. "He was cast out of his fairy colony for pursuing…unnatural magics, but he sought still greater power. He searched every fairy and human archive he could find, until one day he and the would-be alchemist crossed paths. The alchemist believed Maraile's intentions were to give him the power he always sought, but the fairy saw only one thing: a naive child he could manipulate into giving him everything they wanted. And they came so close, this was the medieval era of human history, they had little that could withstand true dark magic.

"Eventually Maraile and his servant found themselves a hiding place in an island off the coast of modern-day Italy. Between the cold weather, nightmarish seas and the magic that protected it their position seemed unassailable, he'd found a way to make the island impossible to approach by sea. But the leaders of the greatest fairy cities joined forces, and with an army of human and fairy soldiers alike they assaulted the fortress.

"But ultimately Maraile brought about his own demise: At the height of his powers his ally saw him for what he really was and tried to flee, Maraile took exception to this and attempted to kill him…but Maraile had trained him too well. Engaging in a magical duel, when the allies finally found their way to the throne room they found the human dead, and Maraile turned into something akin to a husk. He had forgotten the key lesson about dark magic, power like that comes at a cost, one you must be willing to pay."

"This is a fascinating story," Scott said, interrupting. "But I am not sure what links this to this…Ravenspire place."

"The enemy may have been effectively dead," Selina said. "But he possessed artefacts and spells that could not be allowed to remain accessible to just any casual visitor. Somewhere needed to be found that would be difficult, if not impossible, to locate. No-one is quite sure what purpose the Spire served before that time, indeed there's almost no history of it that can be located anywhere, but someone suggested it as it was a fortress in the middle of a mountain range with a massive central tower. It was so difficult to reach it was a unanimous choice, and soon any possessions that had been in Maraile's fortress had found its way to the Spire. For several centuries human and fairy alike acted as envoys, visiting the Spire to ensure that the fortress was still secure. The last time this happened was sometime in the 16th Century, when a representative from the Vatican accompanied a Pixie, but a journey that should have taken them a week and a half was done in less than two days. They returned to the Vatican claiming they could not locate the Spire. Nothing has been heard from the Ravenspire since those days, at least until now."

"A treasure trove of ancient dark magic welcoming god only knows who," Izzy said after a few moments of silence. "Okay, now I understand why you're worried about what is going on here. What are our options?"

"We don't even know where to begin," Selina replied. "The Spire's location was kept hidden from all but a handful of fairies and humans, and if it is written in a book, I am not aware where its location is. If we're going to find it, especially before anyone less…savoury does, we will have to work quickly."

"Let Izzy help you," Terry said. "Assuming she doesn't mind, her research skills may be of some use to you in this situation, and I have plenty of staff who can cover her role. If this situation is as serious as you are saying, this needs to come first."

"The President is right," Nareena said after a moment. "We need to discover the link between the Spire and this girl's death. I would offer a word of caution however: dark magic is not something to be trifled with, tread *extremely* carefully, we cannot be certain what secrets await us, let us hope we do not regret seeking answers to this question."

Once we had attended the banquet and said farewell to the dignitaries we made our way to a room beneath the old library, which contained the books they were unable to find a place for within the main body of the library. Waiting for us there, sat in front of a laptop and staring intently at its screen, was Izzy. She looked up as we reached the bottom of the stairs, smiling broadly at us and beckoning us over.

"I'm amazed you can get any kind of internet connection down here," Mickey said as we reached her. "I hadn't even thought to try."

"This is a fairy city, not the middle of the Sahara Desert," Izzy said, stifling a laugh. "Although the fact they installed electrical supply here after the war helps, a lot. I need to introduce you to someone." She turned the laptop around to reveal a man who didn't look much older than 20, with unkempt ginger hair and a superhero-themed t-shirt matched by the myriad posters covering the walls of his room. "This is Spyke, I thought he could help us on our little fact-finding mission, at least in the human world."

"A pleasure to meet you all," Spyke said in a thick Texan drawl. "What Isabella here is forgetting to mention is why she knows me. I'm a computer hacker."

"*Ex* computer hacker," Izzy said, shooting him a look of mock disapproval. "He works for the US government on improving cyber security nowadays. More relevantly though he's managed to trace our mystery dead girl's identity, and it makes…interesting reading."

"In what sense?" I asked as the others found chairs for us all to sit on.

"Her name is Madeline Curtis," Spyke said as Izzy brought up an image I immediately recognised as the girl I had seen earlier that day. "Up until about three years ago she led a pretty unremarkable life: aced near everything at school, was adored by everyone at school and in the community. If her life had continued like that you guys would likely have never heard of her, but then the hallucinations started."

"The hallucinations?" Mickey asked, raising an inquisitive eyebrow.

"It's pretty hard to track down what happened," Izzy replied. "But there was some kind of incident during a school holiday…whatever happened her life began to suffer. Her grades fell, she stopped talking to friends and her mental health deteriorated without any apparent explanation. Eventually, when she talked about not wanting to carry on, her parents ran out of options and finally called a specialist in teenage mental health, who knew a specialist hospital they could refer her to. Hell, they even offered to pick her up to save the parents the torment of having to drive her there. If you don't bother digging, you could be forgiven for thinking her story ends there."

"Why am I getting a *really* bad feeling about where this story going?" I asked nervously.

"Because the people who picked her up were not who they appeared to be," Spyke replied. "I sent you the link to an article."

Selina clicked on the link and we all gathered round.

MYSTERY OVER MISSING TEENAGERS DEEPENS

The FBI have voiced increasing concern for the safety of several missing teenagers after parents revealed a disturbing element. All had been referred to psychiatric hospitals, but Madeline Curtis' parents especially claim to have handed her to an ambulance crew, but no attempts to find a trace of said crew has turned up any results.

Selina grimaced. "The rest of it is mostly just repeating variations of that paragraph or how to contact the authorities with information."

"Spyke managed to find the notes from one of the counselling sessions she took part in," Izzy said as she passed the file to Selina. "Can you make heads or tails of what she's talking about?"

"I don't know why you'd…" Selina started saying before the words died on her lips. "Oh…oh no."

"What does it say?" Mickey asked.

"Most of it is pretty standard counselling responses," Spyke replied. "What matters is when she is asked to explain what her hallucinations were about. And I quote: 'The little people are in the garden, they are getting nearer and nearer the house, some have even reached the windows. I think they fear our dog but...he cannot hold them forever, they will overcome him and then they will come for me. The little people are coming for me.'"

"The little people," Selina said, audibly shaking. "That term is more of an insult than most people would realize. It is a term for fairies. Clint...whatever happened to her, however she ended up at this city...it's our fault."

On the other side of the Atlantic, in a small town outside Chicago, a young man in a well pressed black suit with short blonde hair, and a pair of sunglasses hiding his eyes, walked up to a well-kept house in a busy suburb. As he reached the door he seemed to pause, as if unsure how to proceed, before knocking three times. At first there was no response, but after a few moments the sound of shuffling footsteps could be heard from inside and shortly the door opened to reveal a small, middle-aged woman in a flowery dress with freshly straightened red hair.

"Whatever you're selling I'm not interested," she said. "I thought I made that clear the last time anyone knocked on my door."

"Apologies ma'am," the young man said, attempting a friendly smile, before taking a card from an inside pocket and showing it to her. "Agent Perkins of the FBI, I'm here to ask you about your daughter's disappearance."

"I thought the investigation was closed," the woman said, giving him a strange look. "Why are you here dredging up bad memories?"

"Mrs Turner—"

"Please, if you're going to be talking about my daughter you may as well call me Elvira."

"Elvira," the man said, trying to hide his frustration at the interruption. "My…superiors believe there may be evidence we have not considered, I am part of the team who are reopening it. I'd just like to ask you a quick question: before her disappearance, or even after it, did you notice anything…unusual about your daughter's room."

"Not that I remember," Elvira said after thinking for a few moments. "Should I have noticed something?"

"It's probably nothing," Perkins replied. "After all you would know your daughter far better than we would. Thank you for your time, I'll make sure we keep you updated if we receive any news. Good day ma'am," he said, bowing before turning away and heading towards the street, looking for a moment before crossing. As he did so he removed his sunglasses, revealing a pair of intense violet eyes, before walking up to a black saloon and climbing in, a pair of slender wings materialising behind his back. "She says she knows nothing."

"You actually believe her?" asked the female fairy in the driver's seat. She had spiky red hair, jade-coloured eyes and wore a long white dress. "After everything humans have done to us you take *her* word for it?"

"The mother speaks the truth," came a voice from the shadow-cloaked rear seat of the car. "She has no idea of what really happened with her daughter, but…" There was a pause as a slender hand, a gold bracelet at its wrist, was placed on the glass of the rear window facing the house.

Suddenly the view on that side of the car turned a dark blue, only the outline of the house and its surroundings visible, other than a circle of orange that shone from one of the upstairs rooms. "But there is something there, that much is certain."

"What would you have us do?" 'Perkins' said.

"Merzel, we must access that room," the shadowy figure replied. "Wait here until nightfall and then find a way into the room. Under *no* circumstances are you to disturb or attack the occupants, we cannot risk raising the alarm among these humans. Petra and I will return to our hiding place and plan our next move."

"Are you sure this is a good idea?" Petra asked, after Merzel stepped out of the car, as the car pulled away from the curb.

"I am not sure of anything," the figure replied as he removed his hand and the view returned to normal. "But if the Spire is open once again, we will not be the only ones hunting, and in that Spire…lies the greatest fairy treasure of all. The truth about magic."

Chapter 3

"We've got to be missing something," Mickey said, after a few moments of us all sitting in stunned silence. "Even assuming what she said was true...fairies wouldn't attack humans, if this was Feth'rael we'd know. Wouldn't we?"

"Your naivety is adorable darling," Selina said, squeezing his hand lightly. "But Feth'rael isn't the beginning and end of evil in the fairy world. However organised the Fae Council made the fairy race look, outside of colonies fairies are largely left to their own devices. If there were real fairies threatening her, without having a way of identifying them ourselves, trying to figure out what this means is going to be no easy task."

"There's worse," Spyke said nervously. "I haven't finished cross-checking the systems, but...I've found at least fourteen near identical cases, even down to how they were abducted, there's a chance these were connected in some way."

"Spyke, send us a list of the names you've found," Selina said, standing up. "Bear with me guys, I'll be back in a minute." With that she suddenly vanished.

"I've spent a year travelling with her," Mickey said, laughing. "And yet that vanishing trick *still* catches me off-guard. What do we think she's looking for?"

"This," Selina said as she reappeared, a book tucked under her arm. "Don't worry, I asked the librarian again before I took this." She opened it on the desk in front of them, stopping at a long list of names. "What would you say if I told you someone kept a list of all the children the Guardians had been ordered to protect?"

"There's only one problem," Izzy said, looking between the book and the list of names on the screen from Spyke. "Unless I'm mistaken, none of the names on this list match up with the names on these books. They weren't targeted because you guys were watching them."

"Then why?" I asked. "What did fourteen ordinary human kids do to get abducted?"

"Their visions," Selina answered, realization spreading across her face. "I don't think they imagined anything, I think they saw something…something they weren't supposed to. What's the best way to discredit something like this?"

"Make everyone think anyone who saw it is delusional," I replied. "Oh my god, someone's been planning this. I'd take a bet that it's not an accident this girl turned up with the note about the Ravenspire. But why?"

"We'll have to talk to the families," Izzy replied. "There may be something they know that the authorities weren't aware of, at the very least something they didn't mention because they thought it wasn't relevant." She found herself suddenly yawning. "God, okay, our first priority I think is sleeping, it's late."

"Izzy's right," Selina said, realising all of us suddenly looked exhausted. "Sorry about this Spyke, we'll have to get back to you in the morning. We promise we won't wake you up *too* early."

"Darling, you can wake me up any time," he managed to say before Izzy abruptly ended the call.

"Sorry about that," Izzy said, closing the laptop lid. "I adore Spyke, but…as you probably just spotted, tact isn't his strong point. Back here tomorrow morning then?"

"Let's get a good night's sleep," Selina said as we all stood up. "Something tells me this mystery's going to get more complicated before we get a straight answer."

Although Niana fell asleep not long after we had got into bed, I found myself unable to sleep, so ended up taking a stroll out to one of the balconies on the upper floors of the tower. While I tried to maintain a relative calm appearance on the outside, adjusting to being the fiancé of the sister of the Queen was easier said than done. But, even with the first signs of trouble now I couldn't imagine being anywhere else at that moment.

I had been expecting to be alone. So I was surprised to find Selina leaning on the rail, staring across the silent, moonlit city below. I leant on the rail next to her, sensing it was best to allow her to speak first, rather than intruding on her silent contemplation.

"My mother used to say that there was only friendship

between our two races," Selina said after a few moments of silence. "Or, at least, before humans turned their backs on fairies that was all there was. But if what Madeline said was true…there are fairies who are attacking humans, ones without the excuse of the god of the dead for why they'd take such action."

"We'll figure this out," I said, squeezing her hand gently as an attempt at reassurance. "I have no intention of letting these kids or their families not find some kind of justice here."

"I hope Niana knows what a lucky woman she is," Selina said, smiling. "But that still leaves us with a baby fairy whose origins we don't have the first idea of. It could have parents out there somewhere, but right now unless they suddenly turn up on our doorstep, we have no way of even knowing where to begin."

"There's got to be something," I said, rubbing my chin thoughtfully. "Maybe we can ask the Queen in the morning, maybe she knows something we don't."

"Not unless she…" Selina's eyes suddenly lit up as she slammed her fist against the rail. "Damnit, how could you be so stupid Selina? Clint, come with me, we need to wake a few of the others up and go to Desh'ayi's room."

"What's going on?" I asked as she reached the door.

"I'll explain when we get to the room," she replied. "I might have a way to answer at least one question we face."

In no time at all Selina and I had been joined by Crystal, Mickey, Nikkela, Niana and the Queen, finding a slightly irritable Desh'ayi looking unimpressed at our presence, while the young fairy simply watched us curiously.

"You're lucky this little one was already awake before you arrived," Desh'ayi said. "Otherwise I'd be putting a sleeping spell on you all right now. What brings you here in the twilight hours?"

"Selina believes she may have a way to discover the child's origins," Nareena replied. "But she insisted she get your permission first."

"Permission for *what* exactly?" Desh'ayi asked, turning her attention to Selina, one eyebrow raised.

"A few years ago, I met an ageing fairy exile," Selina replied. "She avoided suspicion among the human populace by pretending to be a fortune teller. What she never told her customers was the reason her fortunes were so accurate was her magical abilities, including future sight."

"Are you saying you can see into the future?" I asked. "How is that going to help us in this situation?"

"Okay, for one thing I can't see the future," Selina said, letting out an embarrassed laugh. "Of more relevance to this situation is the ability to link minds with another, but those with the ability are not supposed to use it without asking the other's permission first. I clearly cannot ask the child, so you are the next best option."

"Will it harm her in any way?" Desh'ayi asked.

"I promise if I thought it would do any harm I would not even suggest this," Selina replied. "But if you are not happy to let this go ahead, we will find another way."

"I will allow it," Desh'ayi said after a few moments.

"But if it appears either of you are in danger, I will make sure that you are separated as swiftly as possible."

"If you hadn't suggested that, I'd have asked it anyway," Selina said, before walking over to the young fairy and kneeling in front of her. "Hello youngling, is it okay if I take your hand?" As she asked a small hand reached out to her, Selina taking it gently. Suddenly the young fairy's eyes turned silver, and both seemed to be whispering to each other.

"Anyone know if this is supposed to happen?" Mickey asked, looking uneasy. "This feels a bit too weird, even by fairy standards."

"I'm afraid even I don't know how these work," Nareena replied. "It is not magic I believe has happened in this city in a long time, if ever." Suddenly Selina fell back slightly, the fairy's eyes returned to their normal colour. "Are you okay Selina?"

"Get me a piece of paper and Izzy's laptop," Selina replied, as Mickey helped her to her feet. "I saw something in the child's mind...I need to see if Spyke recognises it, it seems familiar to me, but I can't place where it's familiar from."

"Here," Izzy said, putting the laptop on the table and giving Selina the paper and a pen she'd found, before setting about calling Spyke. "I hope we're not interrupting anything," Izzy said as Spyke appeared, a can of beer in one hand.

"Not anything that matters," Spyke said, smiling. "How can I help you?"

"Spyke, do you recognise this place?" Selina said,

showing the picture to us before turning it to the screen. It showed a large lake surrounded by dense woods, with a mountain the distance, and scattered fairy buildings in the foreground.

"You *don't* recognise it?" Spyke asked, raising an eyebrow. "It's the expert hunters favourite holiday location. It's called Lake Wolff, it's in north-eastern Oregon, but there's next to nothing around it. A hunter's lodge, a couple of farmhouses, nothing that resembles that image. Is there anything else I can help you with?"

"Not for now," Selina replied. "We'll speak again soon." She shut the chat and put her head in her hands. "Great Gaia, we're finding more questions than answers."

"What is it?" Mickey asked, walking over and putting an arm around her. "What's wrong?"

"There are fairy colonies in most American states," Selina replied. "But, for some reason, not Oregon. There have only ever been exiles and the occasional fairy living among the humans. This picture...it's either a false memory, or someone has been lying. What could possibly make people or fairies lie about this?"

"You need to go to America," Nareena said. "I don't know whether you'll find all the answers there, but at this point in time it seems that's where all the clues are leading. I would advise resting however."

"The Queen is right," Selina said. "Go back to bed everyone, I guess it's time for me to give you a little tour of my home turf."

Chapter 4

The next day, after we had had a decent night's sleep and some breakfast, Selina teleported me, Niana, Crystal, Nara and Mickey to New York, an odd experience because our relatively rural surroundings swirled around us, to be replaced by a bustling city. We must have been in one of the suburbs as there were no immediate landmarks I could recognise. Once we had materialised Selina started walking towards one of the nearby apartment blocks.

"I hate to question your motives Selina," Mickey said, looking a little embarrassed. "But that image you saw was in Oregon, and none of the missing lived anywhere near New York, so what exactly are we doing here?"

"Before we do anything else we need to visit an old friend of mine," Selina said as she headed down a set of stairs towards the basement. "He tends to know more about what's going on with magic in America than I do most of the time."

"You never mentioned him before," I said as the rest of us followed them down to a narrow passage at the end of which was a heavy-looking wooden door.

"Well, he's not the kind of topic which comes up in just any conversation," Selina said as she reached the door, knocking on it. There was no response forthcoming at first. "C'mon Spira you old con merchant, if you were asleep half of New York would be able to hear you snoring."

"What kind of lowlife would ever—" a voice started saying from the other side of the door, before stopping as the screen across the peephole parted. From where I was stood, I couldn't see anything of the building's occupant, but we could all hear a loud chuckle ring out. "Selina, I should've known it was you from the poor attempt at an insult, of course you can come in."

The screen slammed shut, and for a matter of seconds nothing seemed to change, but then the sound of moving gears could be heard, followed by the door creaking open. We all followed Selina inside, but I couldn't avoid a gasp escaping my lips at my surroundings. There barely seemed to be an inch of free space, the floor was covered in pieces of paper, the walls were covered with shelves full of books, and the desk in the centre of the room carried more books and what appeared to be a Rubik's cube, except this example shone gold.

What caught most of our attention however was the figure sat behind the desk: he was short, rotund and had green, wart-covered skin, a small pair of spectacles perched on the end of his nose.

"You'd think these kids had never seen a goblin before," Spira said, laughing. "They *have* seen a goblin before, haven't they?"

"Most of these 'kids' didn't even know magic existed

prior to a year ago," Selina said, chuckling. "I was working up to introducing the world of goblins."

"In fairness I steer clear of my kind most weeks myself," Spira said, smiling a toothy grin. "But let's cut the crap fairy, you never make social calls to me, what do you *really* want?"

"We need you to find something," Crystal replied. "Specifically we need to find a fairy city."

"A city?" Spira asked, raising an eyebrow. "And what about a dodgy goblin in lower New York makes you think I know where a fairy city would be?"

"Because you know things about the magical world most fairies don't," Selina replied. "And I have reason to believe Lake Wolff in Oregon is home to something I was told doesn't exist?"

"Wolff?" Spira asked, his smile vanishing suddenly, as he jumped off his chair. "I can't help you, if you want help, you'll have to go elsewhere."

"Selina should've added dishonest to her description of you," Nara scoffed.

"Only Selly gets to insult me," Spira snapped back. "And trust me, I'm doing you a favour not telling you what's there. If you can't take that you're welcome to leave."

"What if we paid you?" Mickey asked, rummaging in his pocket to try and find money.

"Take it from me kid," Spira replied. "There is nothing you can *possibly* offer me that would loosen my lips."

"Maybe I can," Marek said as he materialised in the room so suddenly Spira nearly fell over a nearby stack of papers. In one hand I could just make out something that was glinting with the light coming from the window at the other end of the room. "Sorry Selina, I should've asked your permission before coming here."

"You didn't tell me you knew a Sidhe, Selina," Spira said, his grin suddenly returning.

"Half Sidhe," Selina said grumpily. "And he isn't supposed to be here right now."

"I'm sorry Selina," Marek said, giving us an apologetic smile before turning back to Spira. "But just after you left, we found something among the orphan's clothes, I think Spira might be able to help us figure out what it is." He handed it over to Spira, who sat on his chair and picked up a strange magnifying item, like a microscope which could fit over his eye. He let out an audible gasp as he looked at the object. "You know what it is don't you?"

"I can't help you," he replied, placing the item back on the desk and jumping off his chair again.

"I've never known you to give up that easily Spira," Selina said, looking puzzled at his reaction.

"I said *I* couldn't help you," Spira said, letting out a laugh. "Luckily for your little mission, I know someone who can. How familiar are you with the Dragonfire casino in Las Vegas?"

"Oh, it just *had* to be there didn't it," Selina said, rolling their eyes before turning to the rest of us. "Dragonfire is run by a group of...not entirely legitimate goblin businessmen, not that most humans are aware of its real purpose." They turned back to Spira. "Which lowlife ex-buddy of yours are you sending us to Spira?"

"I feel personally slighted by your choice of words there Selly," Spira replied, pretending to be offended, before letting out a chuckle. "It's not one of the goblins: there's an old fairy who rents a room out there, she persuaded me to help her move her stuff into the casino when she first moved in." He picked up the item, which I could now see was an amulet, upon which was an image of a dragon flying above a stretch of water, the dragon's image perfectly reflected in the water. "Unless this is some weird coincidence, I would take a bet she'll know what you're looking for."

"Thank you Spira," Selina said, curtseying to him. "You were as helpful as always, but we'd be stuck if we hadn't asked."

"You should have dinner with me when you get back," Spira said, bowing to us all but giving her a cheeky smile.

"I'm flattered Spira," Selina said, taking Mickey's hand. "But I'm not sure my boyfriend would appreciate me dating other men." She couldn't help laughing at the stunned look on his face. "See you around Spira."

When we teleported a short time later, we found ourselves in a relatively isolated part of Las Vegas, which at first seemed to be the last place I would expect to find anything genuinely magical, until I realized we were stood opposite a large casino. It seemed almost indistinguishable from the other casinos at first glance, until I looked closer and noticed there was a dragon resting above the main entrance, a sight which seemed to surprise everyone other than Selina.

"Is that an *actual* dragon?" Crystal asked, raising an eyebrow.

"You think they'd put a real dragon in the middle of

Las Vegas?" Selina asked, stifling a laugh. "From what I've heard the goblins who run the place put it up because they thought it'd look more appealing to humans. You'd have to ask them how well that plan worked."

"How are we going to get in there?" Mickey asked, looking at the bouncers guarding the entrances. "None of us are twenty-one, we're never getting past those guards."

"Luckily we have a secret weapon," Selina replied. "We're not gambling, and we've got the wings to prove we have business in there. Let's just try and avoid doing anything that may draw unwanted attention from the owners, okay?"

We crossed the empty highway, across the considerable courtyard that lay in front of the casino, before reaching the guard stood outside the entrance, who eyed us all with suspicion for a moment before catching sight of Nara.

"What is a Pixie doing so far from home?" the guard asked, smiling. "I haven't seen one of my kin here in twenty years."

"I knew there was something familiar about his appearance," Nara said, laughing as well. "I'm amazed you were allowed out of Cornwall considering what my mother is usually like about allowing people beyond her borders."

"You two can catch up later," Selina said, I hoped more forcefully than she had intended. "We've been told there's someone here who can locate a fairy city for us, but we weren't told her name or where in the casino we could find her."

"Hmm," the guard said, looking thoughtful for a moment. "That sounds like Madame Anera, she's on the ground floor just past reception. Just tell the guard outside who sent you to her, if she wants to talk, you'll know pretty quickly."

"Thank you," Nara said, curtseying before leading us through the doorway.

Inside the place was teeming with life, of just about every variety of fairy we had met, and a few whose origins I couldn't guess. Flitting between them were sprites who seemed to be sprinkling some kind of dust over some of the drinks, and goblins who were taking payment from some of the customers. We weaved our way through the crowd, the other guests seeming too fascinated by their own conversations to pay any real attention to our presence. Finally, we made it past reception to a short corridor, at the end of which a curtain hung across a doorway, in front of which was stood an especially burly looking fairy with long blonde hair, a scar running across one of his green eyes, and a long red cloak hung over a brown tunic and black trousers. His reaction was the opposite of that we had found when first entering the building, moving a spear to block our path and grimacing at us.

"I believe you children took a wrong turn somewhere," the fairy growled. "Why don't you go back where you came from?"

"You can't talk to us like that," Marek replied angrily. "We have as much right to be here as you do."

"Maybe you should learn to control your whelps," the fairy said, pointing the spear dangerously close to Marek. "He needs to learn to respect his elders."

"Why don't you pick on a fairy your own size," Crystal

said, moving quicker than any of us had noticed and pinning the guard against the wall, her sword placed to his throat. "We have no interest in a fight, we seek an audience with Anera."

"Let them pass old friend," came a voice from beyond the curtain. "They have piqued my curiosity."

Crystal let him go, moving the curtain aside so that we could step inside, letting it fall back as she was the last to enter the room. It was a large library, the walls covered in shelves full of books, but at the centre of the room was a table surrounded by chairs, at the opposite end of which was a large armchair containing possibly the oldest fairy I had ever seen. She was hunched over, eyes seemingly shut beneath wiry grey hair, a shawl pulled over a navy-blue dress. The only sound in the room was her breathing.

"Who was that who was speaking?" I asked, looking around and feeling confused. "She looks like she sleeps more than the average cat."

"Be careful insulting your elders, child," said the old woman, as an apple floated up the table towards the old lady, her eyes suddenly wide open. "Most people don't even know I'm here, what could you possibly want with me?"

"Spira the goblin sent us," Selina replied. "He said you would know the answers we sought."

"Spira?" the elder fairy asked, letting out a laugh, followed by a cough. "That old rogue, what did you show him that required *my* assistance?" As she asked that she gestured towards the chairs, which we all took gladly.

"Not even two days ago a small fairy appeared at the gates of our city," Marek said, taking the necklace from under his tunic. "It was carrying little other than its clothes and this necklace." As he went to put it on the table it started to float towards the old fairy, who watched it closely before taking it in her hand. After a few moments she let out a gasp. "You recognise it, don't you?"

"Surely you all do?" Anera asked, looking between all of us. "*All* fairies should know this logo."

"I have read most of the fairy histories at least once," Selina replied. "None of them contained that image."

"I hadn't thought I was *that* aged," Anera said as she got out of her seat, scanning the shelves. "Great Gaia, the fae are losing their heritage the more we bond with humans," she muttered. "I speak of the greatest fairy city to have ever existed."

"How do you know about the Shadow Glade?" Mickey asked.

"You think *that* the greatest city to have ever existed?" Anera said, turning so she could fix her gaze on Mickey. "Evidently I need to educate you all." She waved a hand and a large tome floated from the highest shelf into her hands, before she walked over and retook her seat. "Are you ready for a story?"

"What kind of story?" Marek asked excitedly.

"One which used to be told to all fairy children," Anera replied, putting the book on the table. "The story of the fortress city of the Americas, the story of Glasswater."

A pickup truck pulled up on the eastern shore of Lake Wolff, at the end of a dirt road isolated even from the low buildings of the farm further up that shore. Once the engine had stopped three men, dressed in khaki clothes, baseball caps and each carrying guns stepped out.

"I still don't get it," Jack, the shortest of the three who had a shock of red hair and piercing blue eyes, said. "There's a forest full of animals on the *other* side of Wolff, the hell are we doing on *this* side?"

"That's *why* we're here," Frank, the tallest of the three with blonde hair tied into a ponytail at the back and a thick beard, replied. "How many animals do you think are left that side that aren't either protected by rangers or hunted by someone else. No-one will think to look here, and I'm pretty sure the Hudlins aren't in their lodge right now."

"What do you think Tam?" Jack asked, turning to the other member of the trio, who was taller than him but considerably stouter. His hair was cut short enough that only the occasional strand of black hair was visible underneath his cap, in contrast to a thick moustache. "What's so interesting?" he asked, noticing Tam was facing away from them.

"I've found something already," Tam said quietly, indicating for them to approach him as he raised his shotgun and pointed towards the creature that had caught his attention: in the midst of tall grass was a bird which was an exceptionally bright red, other than a pair of silver wings, evidently mid-hunt. "You ever seen a bird like that?"

"Who cares," Jack replied, scoffing. "That'll make us a pretty dollar, take it out Tam."

"I was just about to," Tam said, grinning as he raised his gun and pulled the trigger…but nothing happened other than a loud click. "The hell?" He took a cursory look at the gun, but nothing changed.

"Obviously your gun's not as good as you thought it was," Jack said, laughing as he raised his revolver…but the same thing happened again. "Frank?" Frank shook his head. "I can believe one of us forgot to load his gun, but all three of us? Something funny is going on here."

"Lucky I brought us a backup plan then," Frank said, pulling a knife from his belt. "C'mon boys, it can't outrun all three of us." They had gone no more than five steps before they felt a sudden dizzy spell, and when their senses returned to normal, they found they were suddenly among the blades of grass, the grey sky above just visible between what now seemed like a canopy above them. "I think we had one drink too many last night," Frank said, letting out a laugh.

"This ain't drink," Jack said, beckoning them to follow him as they walked into a clearing bordered by a large wooden gate which was partially open and a stone wall which vanished into the grass beyond. "This is that fairy magic everyone's been talking about. I never knew you could find it around here."

"Yeah right," Tam said, letting out an obnoxious laugh. "If this is fairy land, where are they?"

"They're just waiting for the right encouragement," Jack said, stepping towards the gate as he raised his voice and turned back to the other two. "Who wouldn't want to help us hunt that bir—" Jack's sentence ended abruptly, the blade of a knife suddenly visible through his chest. He only had a moment to give his friends a pleading look before his body toppled to the floor.

"This place is a madhouse," Tam said wildly, turning and attempting to flee back the way they had come, but an arrow through his back saw him meet a similar fate to Jack, leaving Frank suddenly alone in the clearing.

"Whoever you…you are," Frank said, trying to raise his pistol, but finding his arm was nowhere near steady enough to be a threat. "We mean you no harm, please don't kill me."

"Interesting," came a voice from beyond the gate, quickly revealed as a fairy in a tattered grey cloak covering black armour, spiky silver hair half covering his grey eyes, and a silver blade similar to the one that had killed Jack sheathed at his belt. Just visible in the air around him were four intricate wings. "I hadn't thought humans so weak as to beg for mercy, or perhaps you've realised your mistake in trespassing on sacred lands."

"We…we didn't know you were here," Frank stammered, finding he was suddenly unable to move. "We meant no disrespect. I'll do whatever you ask, I can keep secrets easily."

"An interesting proposition," the fairy said, walking up to him and withdrawing the blade, placing it at Frank's throat. "After all, I couldn't hope to prove you kept your word once you had left here."

"Son, stop this," came a voice from behind the fairy, as the spirit of a woman, dressed in long black robes, her hair a similar colour, appeared suddenly. "Enough blood has been spilt here, let him go, he is no threat to us. None of them were."

"It is true that death stalks this place," the silver-haired fairy said, staring back into Frank's terrified gaze. "And after all, our races are supposed to be friends now, aren't they?" he asked, offering what seemed a friendly smile, as he leant near to Frank's ear. "Unfortunately for you," he said, stabbing Frank through his heart in a flash, "the wraiths of this place have not been sated." He pulled the blade out, allowing Frank's body to collapse to the floor, walking past the spirit to retrieve the other knife. "Do you have any other...'advice' to offer me mother?"

"You have no idea what sleeps here," his mother replied. "You haven't learnt from your father's mistakes, I don't know what will happen if it is unleashed again."

"That is not my problem," her son responded angrily. "We will have our revenge, the ravens will not forget what happened here, *no-one* will."

Chapter 5

"The story of Glasswater goes back a considerable way," Anera said, after getting her guard to get us all refreshments. "Precisely how long fairies have existed in America is as much a matter for discussion as how long you humans have been here. But eventually they found the same problem humans did: North America is huge, making communication between fairy colonies next to impossible if they were on opposite sides of the continents. That is why a series of *Arth'ila* were founded." She seemed pensive for a moment. "The closest human phrase to it would be a...way station. Most were little more than the cities you would find anywhere else in this world."

She fell silent for a few moments, beginning to flick through the book she had taken off the shelf, before stopping and placing it facing towards us. On one side was a dense wall of text in a language none of us could imagine a creature of her age having any ability to read, but on the opposite page was an image of Lake Wolff. It was what was on the near edge of the lake that caused me to gasp loudly.

A city that seemed to cover every inch of the bank, even in the image each building seeming to glint in sharp sunlight.

"I've been to Lake Wolff before," Serena said, her look of astonishment unmistakable. "I would remember if I had seen a city like that."

"When word reached the city of the human pioneers spreading west, they increased the magical shield around the city," Anera said, letting out a chuckle at our amazement at what was being discussed. "They possessed a great many magical skills. They had the Ithizzi, an elite guard of soldiers said to possess greater magical capability than a lot of skilled fairies, arts and crafts that would take your breath away, and some even claimed control of the waters of Lake Wolff itself."

"That sounds perfect," Crystal said.

"A little too perfect," Nara said suspiciously. "A place like that...they don't exist without secrets, I know that from my own experiences."

"You, my young Pixie friend, are very astute," Anera replied. "Most other cities ignored the stories out of not wishing to confront the army of Glasswater directly, but there *were* stories. There were an...exceptionally high number of fairies from the city who began exploring dark magic, becoming outcasts from society, to the point where there were rumours across most of America that there was something under the city causing all this. Unlike the majority of the *Arth'ila*, Glasswater survived the increasing advancement of human society, their magic so advanced that humans could not even accidentally stumble across it."

"All of this is in the past tense," I said. "What happened?"

"No-one is certain," Anera answered. "There are claims all across America as to what really happened. Some say that the population fled the city after some dark event ruined it, some that they simply cut all ties to the outside world and sealed the city off from intrusion. For whatever reason little has been heard from them since they were part of the American Fae Council who debated whether to aid humanity during World War II." She sighed, closing the book. "The fact we turned our backs on humanity at that moment is something we are ashamed of, I can promise you that."

"Wait," Selina said, reaching into her bag and bringing out the same book she had used to show us the image of the Ravenspire we had seen earlier. "That writing looked familiar, but I couldn't think from where till just now." She opened the book, this time to a page she had evidently picked at random, and that's when we all saw it: her book was written in the same handwriting as the one Anera was holding.

"Let me see," Anera said, using her magic to move the book towards her, and opening it up, flicking through the pages, before the colour drained from her face. "This is indeed the same book, but...where Glasswater should be, there is something else entirely. Indeed, I can find no mention of it anywhere in this book."

"How's that possible?" Crystal asked. "They're the same version of the same book, surely they should be identical."

"It concerns me as well," Anera said, frowning. "This is

no misprint, someone has been trying to erase all trace of this city…this requires more than a simple memory wipe spell. You children must be careful." At that moment her guard appeared in the doorway. "Old friend, what is it?"

"The goblins know our guests are here," the fairy replied.

"They knew we were here the moment we entered surely?" Mickey asked. "Why is this a problem?"

"The goblins take exception to humans being in this casino," Anera replied. "Even ones who are part fairy." She fell silent for a moment, evidently deep in thought, before a cheeky smile crossed her face. "I never did like those old fools, make sure their bouncers are…'distracted', I will make sure the children escape this place." Her guard bowed, ducking back through the curtains as she stood up and beckoned us towards a passage we hadn't noticed at the back of the room. As we reached where she was stood, we realized she was in the midst of casting a spell, a portal forming in the air in front of her, which once fully formed showed the courtyard in front of one of the nearby casinos. "I'm sending you here because I believe there are other fairies there, ones who may be able to assist you. However, I get the feeling these fairies are a little less…skilled at disguising themselves than you are."

"Thank you, Mistress," Selina said, pulling her into a hug that Anera enthusiastically returned. "I promise we will get to the bottom of what happened to Glasswater. Hopefully we will see each other again."

"Go," Anera said, shooing us towards the portal, letting

out a chuckle. "You don't want to see me get soppy, it never ends well."

With that we ducked out, finding ourselves under a large tree across the road from a casino that a quick glance told us was nowhere near the Dragonfire. The courtyard was teeming with people, but it only took me a moment to spot the people Anera had been referring to: near a large fountain, which dominated the main square, were a man and a woman in clothes that appeared more like funeral clothes than those of casino customers, and after staring for a few moments I realized the air around them shimmered unnaturally.

"It's something no human would ever pick up on," Nara said, presumably seeing the same effect I was. "All the magic a fairy possesses cannot entirely shield our wings from sight, that shimmer is their wings affecting the air around them." She turned to the rest of us. "So, what exactly is our plan? If we walk over to them as a group they might run the other way, assuming they can't just teleport out before we can get within grabbing range of them."

"I'll go and…introduce myself," Selina said, a wicked grin crossing their face. "I can make them see what I want them to, just prepare yourselves in case they aren't as harmless as they look." Before any of us could question her or attempt to argue she had set off across the road, approaching the pair as a glamorous young woman, the transformation so subtle I was at a loss to explain when it had happened. For a moment the two seemed wary, but eventually followed her. They arrived just in time to find

Nara and Niana stepping behind them, their blades pressed against their backs.

"The hell is going on here?" the male fairy asked. "We get told an old friend wanted to speak to us and we find ourselves suddenly threatened."

"We were told you could help us," I said as calmly as possible, hoping to defuse the tension that was building between my friends and the newcomers. "We're trying to figure out what happened to the city of Glasswater."

"Glasswater?" the female fairy shooting me a confused look. "I have no damn idea what you're talking about, our master sent us to look for information about Caroline Turner."

"Caroline..." Selina muttered before she gasped. "Guys, Caroline was one of the files Spyke sent us, one of the kids who vanished." She turned to the female fairy. "My name is Selina, my friends and I came to America, in part, on the trail of a girl who turned up dead at our city walls after a similar experience to what occurred to the girl you seek."

"How do we know we can trust them?" the male fairy asked his companion, not bothering to make any attempt to hide his dislike of us.

"I'm not sure we really have another option Merzel," the female fairy replied, turning to face Selina. "My name is Petra, Merzel here is my brother. I believe it may be worthwhile us sharing what information we have gathered, but it is not safe to do so here. There is a cafe, the Dark Horse, approximately ten minutes walk from here, we will meet you there shortly." With that, and before any of us could ask any further questions of them, they vanished suddenly.

"Damn teleport magic," Selina said angrily. "I should've known they wouldn't come with me unless they knew they had a way out. What do we think, do we trust these guys?"

"I say we give them a chance," I replied. "I'm thinking if they had any questionable motives, they would have attacked us already, or at the very least they wouldn't pick a public location to have a conversation."

"I'm with Clint," Niana said. "Let's get going before they teleport out of here and we lose any chance of keeping track of them."

We walked to the cafe, deciding that appearing out of thin air would risk too much unwanted attention from the non-fairies around us. In a roadside cafe, sat at a table as far from the windows as could be managed were the two fairies, sat deep in conversation until they caught sight of our approach.

"I'm going to get us a drink," Selina said, heading for the counter before any of us could offer any kind of protest or even request a specific drink. We shuffled over to the table, none of us seeming confident enough to sit too close to the other two fairies. The table was silent until Selina came over with a tray full of drinks, taking a seat between Petra and Mickey and sighing for a moment. "What are you doing looking for Caroline?"

"I could ask you the same," Merzel replied. "Judging by your accents all but one of you is a long way from home, and we're under strict orders to not discuss this with anyone we're not absolutely certain we can trust."

"Brother, this is getting us nowhere," Petra said, sighing. "We are supposed to be helping each other, not arguing about things which in the grand scheme of things couldn't be much less relevant." She turned to the rest of us. "The fairy we work for believes he knows why the young people were targeted, although as of this moment he hasn't told either of us what that explanation might be. Do you know much about what happened to them?"

"All we know is they all went missing around the same time," I replied. "Well, that and they reported variations on the same supposed hallucination. Beyond the similar experiences we can find nothing to actually link any of them." I suddenly had a sense something was wrong, looking around and noticing that no-one else in the room, other than those sat at our table, appeared to be moving. For a moment I was confused, but then I remembered the trick we had used to get uninterrupted access to the Prime Minister. "Did you guys freeze time?" I asked Petra.

"That's not us," Merzel replied. "That kind of magic is extremely difficult, it can't be learned by just anyone." He suddenly stood up, Petra doing the same not long after, both looking towards the back of the cafe. For a moment I couldn't understand what had drawn their attention, but then I saw there was one other occupant of the cafe apparently unaffected by the spell: a tall figure was picking his way through the immobile figures, the hood of a black cloak hiding all but his thin mouth and stubbled chin from our view. Beneath the cloak, he was wearing a tunic and green trousers, but his most notable feature could be found on his wrists: a pair of golden trinkets that stretched from the wrist to somewhere under the sleeve. He waved a hand and suddenly a chair appeared next to our table, which he sat down in, indicating to the siblings to retake their seats. "Master, I thought you were remaining hidden back at the hotel, what brings you here?"

"Because you two are in danger of talking yourselves out of an alliance that would benefit all of us around this table," the newcomer said, before turning to us, pulling the hood back. Unlike Anera the male fairy we were confronted with appeared ageless. His face was a stark white, a pair of grey eyes staring out from underneath furrowed brows, thinning black hair swept back to show a forehead surprisingly free of wrinkles. "My name is Arkelion," the fairy said. "I come from one of the old fairy colonies out in the Rocky Mountains, much like my two associates here."

"While I appreciate you seeming to be so friendly," Selina said. "Best as I can tell you don't know us from Adam, what makes you think you can trust us? Hell, how do we know we can trust *you*? For all we know you're one of the fairies who helped lead to these kids vanishing in the first place."

"That is a sensible response," Arkelion replied, letting out a light laugh. "I would be concerned if you were not suspicious of me Selina." I was about to ask how he knew her name when he put a hand up. "My apologies, one of the first things I do before I meet directly with anyone is scan their minds, to ensure that their good intentions are as genuine as they wish me to believe. I do not give forewarning as the few who have successfully resisted my probes have been those who knew in advance."

"Can we get to the point?" Nara snapped. "I can't help but feel you're not telling us something about this whole situation."

"I assume you have seen the messages about the Ravenspire by now?" Arkelion asked, a troubled look crossing his face as he saw us all nod. "Do you know the story of the fairy city of Azhar?"

"Azhar was where the fallen fairy whose treasures were taken to the Spire made his last stand," Selina replied. "Although I'd describe it as more like a fortress than a city, it was deserted after his death, mainly because there was little of any interest there."

"If only that were true," Arkelion said, reaching under his cloak and placing an object, something akin to an especially chunky frisbee with a football at its heart, onto the table. While the rest was ice blue in colour the ball throbbed with an eerie white colour. "Azhar did not require much encouragement to side with the enemy. They openly practised dark magic and welcomed such a skilled practitioner among them so they could learn more. When they feared Azhar was about to fall, they formed a plan to remove their secrets. These are—"

"The Orbs of the Drakoni…" Nara said, seeming to be staring into the distance until Crystal gently nudged her. "Sorry darling," she said, before turning to the rest of us. "It's a legend among the Pixies, although considering what's sat in front of us, perhaps not as much of a legend as I suspected. They're supposed to be objects of great evil, but my mother barely attempted to explain what she meant by that."

"Drakoni was the name of the cult that lived within Azhar," Arkelion said. "When the enemy fell it is said the Drakoni constructed these devices as a way to ensure the dark magic they discovered was safe, in order to ensure those who tried to stop them couldn't rid the world of their taint entirely. There were fourteen of them, one for each member of the Drakoni inner circle. One was captured not long after and taken to the Ravenspire, another was reported lost at sea, but the others…"

"Clint," Crystal said, feeling her heart sink. "Twelve missing people…twelve orbs…This is pointing in a disturbing direction."

"This particular Orb was found in the bedroom of one of the missing," Arkelion continued. "I share a similar fear to this young lady, these are not items which would end up in human hands by mistake. Combine it with the return of the Spire…someone is putting something into motion, and we can barely begin to guess what it is."

"Why are you here if you suspect this is what we're dealing with?" I asked.

"Because I believe, whatever this is, we are capable of fixing it before the damage is irreversible," Arkelion answered. "While I haven't been able to discover the location of the majority of the missing, I have managed to trace two of them to the same place." He took a folder from under his cloak, throwing it to the centre of the table where we could all see it. "St Jude's Psychiatric Hospital in Idaho, it took considerable digging to track down, but apparently our enemy did not do a perfect job of covering their tracks. At least two of the missing were taken there."

"Look, no offence," Mickey said, sighing. "But this doesn't sound urgent, why should we worry if they're in a secure hospital?"

"Because it is not secure," Arkelion replied, his rising anger detectable despite an apparently calm tone. "Someone has discovered their current location, and is planning to attack the hospital. If there is any chance one of the Drakonian orbs is in that building—"

"We should join forces," I said, interrupting him so suddenly that even Niana, sat next to me, let out a gasp of surprise. "I don't know what we're going to be facing, but I'd take a bet the more people at the hospital, the less innocent people get hurt."

"I'm glad you said that Clint," Arkelion said, standing up. "I advise you leave immediately, I am not sure when the enemy will arrive and I would not waste time unnecessarily. I can promise that, should you need it, my help will be with you in an instant." With that, and before any of us could ask any more questions, or make any other comment, he vanished, the world around us suddenly returning to normal.

"Why do I get the feeling we're going to regret that suggestion?" Niana asked, taking my hand as she stood up. "I don't even know how we're supposed to get to Idaho from here."

"I know," Petra said, a smile playing across her lips.

"But we'd better get out of here, otherwise we risk a lot of unwanted attention from the locals."

Meanwhile, at St Jude's, Mike Thomas was completing his hourly round of the wards, glad to see things were as uneventful as usual. He was about to retrace his steps to go back to the office when his walkie-talkie suddenly burst into life.

"*Mike,*" came Carlos' panicked voice, "*have you finished your rounds yet?*"

"I was just about to make sure the new kid is settling in okay on my way back," Mike replied. "Why do you ask?"

"*I think you'd better come straight back,*" Carlos answered. "*There's a…I'm going to be honest, I'm better off showing you than trying to describe it.*"

"I'll come straight back," Mike said, picking the quickest route back. He knew Carlos was a pretty unflappable character, so the fact he seemed so panicked told him something was very wrong. Within a matter of minutes, he found himself keying himself into the security office, where Carlos was hunched over in front of the security monitor. "Carlos, what's going on?"

"I was doing the regular sweep of the CCTV," Carlos replied, not looking round. "Most of it was the usual fare, but then I checked Room 12 and…" he fell silent, rewinding the tape. As Mike watched he saw a male figure appear by the room's bay window, before vanishing.

"The hell…bring that back on screen and pause," Mike said, stepping nearer once the image was paused on the strange intruder. "How in god's name is someone managing to get in and out of that room without triggering any alarms or having to walk past us?"

"It gets worse," Carlos said. "That's been happening repeatedly in the last half hour." He looked around, noticing Mike was opening the room's safe. "What are you doing?"

"Whoever that is, I can't think he has any good intentions," Mike said, taking out a gun and checking it was loaded. "I'm going in there Carlos, I need you to keep an eye on that room. Anything goes wrong, you call the authorities immediately." He shut the safe again. "I *really* hope this is an unnecessary precaution."

Mike stepped out of the office, tucking the gun under the back of his shirt and heading down the main hallway. He had hoped he could reach his destination unaccosted, but he suddenly heard one of the doors opening.

"M…Mike?" asked a rather timid sounding voice, Mike turning to find Katerina, one of the hospital's more mature patients, peering around the door. "Is everything okay? I thought I heard something."

"I'm sorry if I worried you," Mike said, trying to give her a reassuring smile. "We're just worried about one of the other occupants, we'll be done soon."

He breathed a sigh of relief as the door closed again. He continued down the hall, not stopping until he reached Room 12. Ordinarily he would have knocked, but at that moment he suspected time was of the essence, so attempted to turn the doorknob, but the door didn't budge. His next option was to swipe his card, which at any other time would have resulted in the lock clicking, but nothing happened.

He could hear strange noises, so he took the gun from where he had hidden it. "I'm going to wind up regretting this," he muttered under his breath, aiming the gun at the lock, letting out a sigh of relief as the shot finally forced the door open. He pushed it open, finding the room unoccupied other than the patient he expected to be there, sat bolt upright by the pillows. "Carlos," he said into the walkie-talkie. "What happened to our intruder?"

"*I'm not sure,*" came the reply. "*He vanished from the CCTV just before you reached the doorway.*"

"Her name's Caroline, right?"

"*That's correct,*" came Carlos' response.

"Thanks," he said, walking to the end of the bed and watching the young woman. "Caroline, are you okay?" Caroline looked up, but not uttering a word. "We were worried something had happened in here." For a few moments nothing happened, but then Caroline lifted her right arm, pointing straight at Mike. "Yeah, it's Mike, you remember me, right? You used to like telling me ab..." The words died on his lips as the realization hit him: she wasn't pointing at him, in fact he suspected she couldn't even see him for some reason. He turned around, and felt his heart suddenly sink at what he saw. In the midst of Caroline's writing on the wall was a new message, written in what he had a horrible feeling was someone's blood:

"*The Ravens have marked you,*
Your reckoning has come,
The Drakoni will return,
We're already here..."

"Carlos…" Mike said shakily. "I think it might be time to call the authorities."

"*Why?*" Carlos asked. "*What did you find in that room?*"

"Trouble," Mike replied, still shaking. "We're all in deep, deep trouble."

Chapter 6

Although our journey by teleportation was relatively quick, the number of jumps Petra required us to make seemed to leave even Selina look a little queasy when we finally came to a stop. A look around us revealed that we were at the end of a driveway, at the far end of which was a large, stark white building. I could just make out a sign outside it, but at that distance I couldn't tell what the sign said.

"Was…was that really necessary Petra?" Mickey asked, still trying to catch his breath. "All that effort and we're *still* not at our location."

"We're here," Petra said confidently. "That…effort as you put it, was to put off any potential pursuers. If I had simply teleported us straight here, we may have been ambushed."

"Then why not take us straight inside the building?" Marek asked.

"I think I know why," I replied. "It's the same reason why, when we first sought my uncle's help, we did not teleport straight into his house: if we materialise in the middle of a building without a word of warning there's a good chance we won't get a positive response." I couldn't help hearing a groan from Mickey. "At least we'll get to the facility *alive*, I don't know about you, but I'll take that over an easy journey any day of the week."

The trip up the driveway was less difficult than I had feared, and I noticed out of the corner of my eye that Marek even took to skipping along after we had reached the halfway point, causing me to smile at the joy Marek was showing at that moment. When we finally reached the building, the sign was easily readable: *St Jude's Psychiatric Hospital.* As the curtains seemed to be drawn across the windows the only significant light coming from the building was from Reception, which as we entered was only occupied by a tall man in a security guard's uniform, apparently trying and failing to make a phone call. As he slammed the phone down, he caught sight of us and let out a sigh.

"I hate to break this to you but visiting hours finished about an hour ago," the guard said, turning to us. "You'll just have to come back tomorrow."

"We're not here to visit," Petra said, walking up to counter with more confidence than I was personally feeling. "We need to talk about one of the patients, it's a matter of urgency."

"Well unless you're police," the man said, raising an eyebrow, "you'll have to speak to one of the doctors, none of whom are currently available. Shall I escort you from the premises?"

"Petra," I said under my breath as I walked up to her, sensing her anger was threatening to boil over. "Picking a fight with security will help—" I stopped talking as I caught sight of the interior of the nearby security room. A Latino guard was hunched over in front of a security monitor, and although I couldn't make out anything on the screen I could hear the man's reaction, although I doubted he intended it to sound as loud as it was.

"I still don't get how a raven becomes a man..." he mused.

"What did your colleague just say?" Selina asked, appearing next to me.

"That's none of your goddamn business," the guard behind the desk responded angrily, reaching for the phone. "Get out of here before I call the police."

"We do not have time for this," Selina muttered, turning to me and Petra. "Show him," she said, sighing at our confusion. "The wings, show him your wings." We did as Selina asked, the guard behind the desk nearly dropping his phone at the sight.

"Mike, why are there fairies at our front desk?" asked the other security guard, who had now turned to look at us. "Someone want to fill me in here?"

"We will answer your questions if you wish," Petra replied. "But right now everyone in this hospital is in danger, we need to see that security tape."

For a moment Mike seemed to consider his options, before sighing.

"Okay, fine," Mike replied, throwing his hands up in resignation. "But only you three, the rest of you will have to wait out here." He lifted the partition in the desk, beckoning us through to the security room, where his colleague moved aside to give us a clear view. "This man keeps appearing on our cameras, but we can find no trace of him, other than every time he vanishes *that* raven appears on the windowsill."

"Oh Mike…that's not a human," Selina said, the panic in their voice unmistakable. "I don't know whether this is good or bad, but…it definitely complicates things."

"What do you mean not human?" asked the Latino guard, who seemed to let out an embarrassed laugh at the fact we were suddenly looking at him. "I should have introduced myself, my name is Carlos."

"Well Carlos," Selina replied. "It's…not necessarily easy to explain." She sat down in the chair, staying quiet for a moment. "They're called the Raverni, precisely what they are is a matter of debate among the few fairies who know about them. What little is known is they come from the Ravenspire, acting either as its guards, or its messengers, depending on who you believe. No-one is sure whether they're good or bad, but if they're here, we have a problem."

"What about the writing?" Carlos asked. "That had as much to do with why we were trying to contact the police as this…Raven thing did."

"Wait, *what* writing?" I asked, feeling a sense of frustration building.

"I guess I'd better show you," Mike said, grabbing a keyring covered in keys from a hook on the wall. "Stay here Carlos, if you see anything else suspicious you let us know immediately." He turned to us. "Follow me."

After Mike had reluctantly agreed to allow the others to

come with us, we headed through the doors into the east wing, but almost as soon as we stepped onto the ward I had a severe feeling of unease. Though I wasn't sure what I had expected from a hospital like this, a quiet building with patients who seemed to almost be in a zen-like state was not even close to the image in my head. I was so focused on trying to figure out why this place seemed so strange that I was caught off-guard by the sudden loud cough coming from the direction of one of the rooms. A short woman, her hair beginning to show the smallest sign of grey, was peeking around the open door.

"Are…are you fairies?" the woman asked, focusing on Niana especially. "I knew something was going on, despite what Michael said."

"Katerina," Mike said, sighing as he turned to look at the woman. "Now is *not* the time for this conversation, could you go ba—"

"Mike, let me talk to her," Niana said, cutting his sentence short. Before he could make any response, she walked over to Katerina, taking her hand in hers. "You didn't sound surprised, you've met my kind before, haven't you?"

"I'm…I'm not sure," Katerina replied, looking startled at the question. "When I was much younger I certainly saw something, perhaps you would be able to explain it to me?"

"Once this is dealt with, I'd be happy to," Niana replied. "But right now things are potentially dangerous. If you shut the door firmly, I promise my friends and I will get to the bottom of this." That seemed sufficient reassurance for Katerina, who nodded to all of us before going back to the safety of her room. I had to smile at the smug look on Niana's face as she walked back to me, taking my hand and giving it a light squeeze. "I spent all but the last year of my life in a city at war Clint," she said as we started walking again. "My siblings were always the ones who dealt with military matters, my job was to ensure no-one was frightened...even at times when I feared death was near myself. I'm not sure how good a job I ever did with it though."

"Well, if just now is anything to go by you should have more confidence in your talents," I replied, giving her a reassuring smile.

"We're here," Mike finally said, stopping outside a room whose door was a plain white apart from the number 12 attached the door in red lettering. He knocked gently on the door. "Caroline, I'm coming in, okay?" No reply was forthcoming, but he opened the door anyway, beckoning for the rest of us to follow. None of us could stop ourselves from letting out a gasp at the sight that awaited us: While the majority of the room seemed little different from a well-stocked en-suite in a respectable hotel it was impossible to ignore the words that seemed to cover almost the entirety of the walls, never mind the repeated mention of ravens. Sat on the room's single bed was a young woman with tousled ginger hair, who showed no sign of having noticed our arrival in the room. "At first we tried to remove the writing," Mike said, apparently aware of what had grabbed our attention so thoroughly. "But she replaces anything we manage to remove far quicker than we can clean it up, so we gave up eventually. Besides, that's not the writing we need to worry about, *this* is."

We all followed the direction he was pointing, and at the sight of the red writing, standing out against the other writing's black ink, I felt my blood run ice cold. I couldn't pretend to understand what the message meant, but the fact Niana's grip on my hand noticeably tightened was enough to tell me the sense of alarm was not unique to me.

"Great Gaia…" Selina said, kneeling in front of the writing. "This building isn't safe any longer, assuming it ever was."

"What does it mean?" Mike asked.

"I don't understand Selina," Mickey said, resting her hand on her shoulder. "You said the Drakoni were defeated while the Ravenspire was still open, that was more than five centuries ago at this point. No magic should be capable of keeping someone alive that long surely?"

"The original Drakoni wouldn't *need* to be alive," Selina replied, taking Mickey's hand in hers. "This is no ordinary dark magic we're dealing with, all it would need was someone desperate for power and aware of these orbs…crap," she said under her breath, before standing up and walking out of the room, leaving us in stunned silence before following as rapidly as we could.

"We need to evacuate this place," Selina said when we found her at the reception. "Anyone messing with this kind of power isn't going to be afraid of causing collateral damage.

Tell me there's some place we can get them to which is at least relatively safe?"

"I'm not sure," Mike said, grimacing as he leant against the reception desk.

"I know somewhere," Carlos said after a few moments of silence. "There's a house about fifteen-minute drive from here. Originally it was supposed to be quarters for this place's nurses, until they realised only two people could share the house at a time and there was no-one who wanted to stay there. It's not a long-term option, but it'd at least give us somewhere safe for the residents to stay for now. The only thing is, we can't send them out there alone, they'll need an escort."

"Well done for volunteering Carlos," Mike said, patting his colleague's shoulder. "That just made—"

"I'm not volunteering," Carlos said irritably. "You have kids, I don't. We have no idea what's going to turn up here, Mandy would never forgive me if something happened to you." He smiled softly as we all heard a resigned sigh escape Mike's mouth. "I promise if you miss anything exciting, we'll tell you all about it afterwards."

"I suggest Marek goes with you," Selina said. "That way you have some back-up."

"This isn't about back-up," Marek said angrily. "You're treating me like a kid, you just don't trust me to back you up in a fight."

"You *are* still a kid Marek," Selina said, their anger rising as she squared up to him. "We got lucky with Feth'rael, I would take a bet whatever is coming will have no qualms about killing you if they have to. This isn't a negotiation."

"Selina," Niana said, stepping between them. "This isn't going to help anyone." She turned to Marek, bending down so she could look straight into his eyes. "Marek, I know this feels unfair, but however much my sister has trained you, you are not ready for a magical battle. Not a real one anyway. Besides, we can't be sure Mike and the others won't be in danger, they need your help as much as we do, okay?" She smiled as the anger drained from his face and he nodded enthusiastically. "Right, time is of the essence, let's get the civilians out of here before they get caught in the crossfire."

Marek and Mike gathered the residents remarkably quickly, Carlos went with them until he was certain they had all passed through a high security gate at the back of the hospital. By the time he had returned however it was already almost dark, the rest of my group checking our weapons as he approached.

"Do you have anything you can fight with?" Niana asked Carlos, as she gave her short sword a few practice swings. "I'm afraid we didn't think to bring anything extra with us."

"Luckily there is one weird part of the hospital inventory I'm appreciating right about now," Carlos replied, ducking into the security office, before coming back out, a pistol in one hand three ammo clips tucked under his other arm. "Not exactly a military armoury, but then I don't think my bosses…thought…" he suddenly trailed off, looking past us. "Caroline?" he asked, causing all of us to look around, finding the young woman from earlier stood not far from us. "I thought you left the building with the others?"

"I didn't want to evacuate," Caroline said, eliciting a loud gasp from Carlos, making me jump. "Besides, I have skills you may find useful in the coming fight."

"No offence," Mickey said, laughing. "But I don't see what…a…" The words died on his lips as she began weaving magic around her. "Selina, I thought you said she wasn't a fairy?"

"She isn't," Selina replied, and out of the corner of my eye I could see a look of shock on their face. "She's…I didn't think normal humans could wield magic."

"There is an explanation for this," Caroline said, walking over to us. "However, right now we have to worry—" She stopped abruptly as the lights suddenly cut out, plunging us all into darkness. "Carlos, there…there's a way to turn the lights on, isn't there?"

"There should be," Carlos replied. "Give me a minute and I'll find a flashlight, that'll make it a hell of a lot easier to see where I'm going." Just as I heard a metal drawer opening there was a loud thunk from somewhere nearby. I saw Carlos shine a light in the direction of Selina, who had her back to all of us.

"Oh god…" Selina said.

"Selina?" Mickey asked, before we all saw what had caught her attention. Dozens of pairs of red eyes were suddenly visible in the darkness around us. "Darling, what is this? What's going on?"

For a few seconds it seemed none of us could think of anything to say, before I could hear a weapon being drawn from Selina's direction, the silence suddenly broken by Selina themselves:

"They're here."

Chapter 7

For a few moments we all seemed to have been stunned into silence. The enemy in front of us also seemed too surprised by our appearance to immediately attack. But the silence didn't last, as I threw myself to the floor barely in time to avoid a burst of blood red magic which slammed into the desk where my chest had been mere moments before. I could just see Petra and Selina exchanging spells with the enemy, the bursts of light occasionally illuminating them, my blood running cold at what little I could see: although their faces could have almost passed for human, their eyes, and indeed their tongues, appeared more akin to snakes.

"Get down!" Selina called out to me.

I didn't need any further encouragement, using a mixture of a skilful jump and my wings to spring over the desk and land slightly clumsily on the floor behind it. Taking stock of the group around me it didn't take long to realise Merzel must be helping Selina and Petra with the fight.

"We need a plan," Niana said, as the other three retreated behind the desk, it dawning on me that there was little cover on the other side. "We can't stay pinned down here, they'll have free run of the hospital."

"We have to restore power," Petra said, throwing a fireball over the desk. "Given the accuracy of their magic, they must be able to see what's happening in the dark, unlike us. I don't suppose you have any useful information, Carlos?"

"Bear with me," the security guard replied, scrambling away from the small circle of light I realised Niana was forming around us. After a few moments he returned, a map of the building in his hands, which he spread on the floor. "Ah. Do you want the good news or the bad?"

"Right now we could do with some good news," Mickey said, jumping up to fire a spell of his own at the attackers before dropping to the floor again.

"The...Orb you mentioned before?" he asked. "I believe I've found the most likely location for it to be in this place."

"And the bad news?" I asked with some dread.

"Oh crap," Petra said, sitting down long enough to see Carlos respond by pointing to a corner of the building that, even to the eye of someone unfamiliar with the facility, was some distance away. "Something tells me our 'friends' out there aren't just going to let us sneak out of the reception area unnoticed."

"It might be past the point we can afford to stand around waiting for an opening," Merzel said, causing me to turn to find, to my surprise, that he was perched on top of the desk, his wings spread wide. "Their last spell gave me enough light to spot that a group of them have broken off for the main attackers and headed deeper into the hospital."

"Crap," Mickey said under his breath. "We were never their target, they're just buying time to find the Orb before we can. We need to do something."

"We're not going to get very far while the power's out of action," Selina said, turning to Carlos. "If we gave you a bit of protection, do you think you could get the fuse box working again?"

"Assuming there's nothing seriously wrong with it?" he asked. "Sure I can. Give me a second," he said, ducking back into the office to where a set of walkie-talkies were sat on the shelf.

"Great," Selina said, grinning. "Petra, you and me will escort him to the fuse box, but we're going to need someone to stop them just whisking the Orb out of here while we're dealing with the electricity situation."

"Leave that to me," I said, before I had taken even a moment to consider whether volunteering for the task was a sensible decision. "As long as I know where I'm going, I should be able to handle whatever I run into on the way."

"I can help with that," Caroline said, letting out a soft chuckle at the look of shock we all caught cross Carlos' face. "The location of this place's lost and found is one of the worst kept secrets in this place Carlos, the only reason you look so surprised is because I happen to be the only patient here who hasn't tried to break into it to retrieve any items."

"I'm going too," Niana said, cutting off any protest from Carlos. "There's no way you two can get through the hospital alone, and I'm not risking you two getting hurt.

There are times to be an action hero, this is NOT one of them."

"And what exactly will the rest of us be doing?" Merzel asked irritably.

"You're going to be keeping them distracted enough the rest of us don't get overrun," Petra said, placing a hand on his shoulder. "Considering they've got us outnumbered, that could be the most important role of all, okay?"

"Damnit sister," Merzel replied, letting out a resigned sigh. "Not for the first time you make an argument I can't counter properly. Fine, I'll follow the plan. But we're going to need a way of keeping in contact, mind links won't run in the midst of battle, not if we're going to fight effectively."

"Then you're in luck," Carlos said, having managed to duck into the office while we were busy talking, returning with several walkie-talkies in his hands. "These are all keyed into the same frequencies, so there's no reason we shouldn't keep in contact while we're off on our missions."

We made our move under the cover of a barrage of magic from Merzel, Mickey and Crystal, Carlos' team heading in the direction of the main ward, while my team headed the opposite way. Niana's magic, and the occasional emergency light, were all that enabled us to see where we were going, passing treatment and common rooms that seemed ominously quiet with everyone evacuated. I occasionally stole a glance at Niana, who offered as close to a reassuring smile as I suspected she felt able to provide.

"How did you discover your magic skills?" Caroline

asked suddenly, making me almost jump out of my skin with surprise. "Clint, I mean," she added. "I can tell Niana is a fairy, but the origins of your powers are more difficult to ascertain."

"I'm a fairy too," I replied. "Well, my mother was. I only really discovered my magical abilities thanks to Niana and her family. How about you?"

"I've always known there was something...different about me," Caroline replied. "I'd know who was going to pick a fight at school before even they knew it, I even once told a friend a boy had a crush on him...before he'd had a chance to tell his parents he was gay. That did not go down well with anyone, but at least they weren't calling me crazy like they did when my parents got me sent here."

"I don't think it's that simple though," I said. "You're not the only young person this happened to, and we have good reason to suspect your parents genuinely believed you would be helped and were tricked by some outside force. Maybe you can help us get to the bottom of what—" My sentence was suddenly cut short as Niana pulled me into a short side corridor that led to what appeared to be a small storage cupboard, placing a hand over my mouth to stop me talking just as Caroline joined us. Niana nodded further up the corridor, where I caught sight of what had alarmed her: Two of the creatures from the entrance hall were deep in conversation, lit by an eerie red light which seemed to hover just above their heads. "What *are* those things? They don't look like fairies."

"Well, I could point out not all fairies look alike," Niana replied, the tone of her voice somewhere between amused and annoyed. "But you're right, their magical aura isn't anything like the fairies I've seen before, but we can worry about that later," she said, nodding in the same direction, where we could just see the pair vanishing out of sight around the distant corner. "C'mon, they've already got a headstart on us, let's not waste more time."

"Just once it'd be nice if we had something simple to deal with," I said with a wry laugh as we started walking again. "We've barely planned our wedding and—" I stopped suddenly something urging me to turn around. Caroline had stopped not far from our hiding place, looking down a corridor that in our rush I hadn't previously noticed.

"Caroline," I said impatiently as I walked back towards her. "We don't have t—" When I reached level with where she was stood, I spotted what had caused her to be distracted. In the middle of the corridor, halfway down it, was what to the untrained eye would appear to be nothing more than a raven somehow trapped in the building by accident. But my magical sensitivity told me this could not be further from the truth. "Niana, you need to see this."

"Well, this is an interesting development," Niana said once she had caught sight of the bird, which had begun to nod its head further down the side passage. She grabbed the walkie-talkie from her belt. "Selina, we've come across something. That Raverni from earlier is back, he seems to want us to follow him. Ordinarily I'd be up for it, but the othe—"

"Do it," Selina's answer came, cutting the explanation short. "The Raverni have as little interest in the Orb falling into the wrong hands, it may well be trying to show you a shortcut. Feel free to keep us updated though."

"Well, let's see where this goes then," I said, wishing I felt as confident as I was trying to sound, although I grabbed Niana's hand so that I could be certain of where she was. However, as we reached where the Raverni was stood the environment around us shifted, and we found ourselves suddenly stood in a corridor which on one side faced out onto a garden enclosed on all sides. "Erm, what the hell just happened?"

"Some form of displacement spell," Niana replied. "But not like any I've ever seen, the ones I've heard of can't be done instantaneously. Apparently the Raverni have a few tricks of their own up their sleeves. I don't know how useful that was though."

"I do," Caroline said suddenly. "It got us exactly what we wanted."

At her comment Niana and I turned around, to discover that the door immediately in front of us was marked 'Patient's Property, Staff Only', a fact that made me smile…until I spotted the other detail about the door. It was already ajar, and there was the sound of items being thrown around inside.

"Be careful," Niana said to me quietly as I stepped towards the door. "Any element of surprise we might have here won't last long if we make a noisy entrance." I simply nodded in response, opening the door quietly. My hand shot to the hilt of my sword almost immediately upon catching sight of what was in the room. Its contents had been thrown all over the floor, from small lockets which couldn't have meant much beyond sentimental value to a massive model ship I felt amazed had survived falling to the floor seemingly unharmed. At the centre of the room, doing their best to either rip apart or break anything they could get their hands on was one of the creatures, but also a young white man in a hoodie and a pair of jeans covered in holes. "Clint, take the kid, I'll deal with the…whatever the hell that thing is."

"Seriously, are you trying to be the most stereotypical rebellious teenager ever?" I asked, stepping towards the boy, who had turned to face me. "It's a good thing we found you and not security."

"You never heard of finders keepers?" the boy snarled. "We got here before you, now get the hell off my turf before you regret it." With that he pulled a gun out of his top, but I could see from how much his hand was shaking he wasn't used to using one.

"You have no idea what you're meddling in do you?" I asked, disarming him with a flick of the hand which sent a pulse of magic through his arm, causing him to flinch. "Look, I don't want to hurt you, get out of here." My satisfaction at the sight of the boy fleeing past me was cut short at the sound of Niana screaming. The other creature had one of its arms tight around her neck, and she was struggling helplessly against its grip. As I tried to move towards her the creature raised its other arm, from which sprouted a pulse of dark energy which stopped barely short of the side of her head. "Let her go," I snarled. "You touch a hair on her head and I—"

"You what?" the creature said, sounding somewhere

between a hiss and a snarl. "Your magic is pitiful, however, I can make a deal with you: give me the Orb and we'll give you all a nice head start before we start killing you."

"That's not much of a deal," I scoffed. "I don't even need to attack you directly, I just nee…" My words trailed off as I saw the creature suddenly shrivelling, its grip on Niana loosening to the point where she could escape his grip and race to my side. "What the hell is happening?"

"I don't know," Niana said, before letting out a gasp as we both caught sight of the stream of gold light leaving the creatures body and winding past us to the doorway. When we turned we found Caroline stood there, one of the Drakoni Orbs held in her arms, the light pouring into it. "Caroline…" Niana said, the fear in her voice audible. "What have you done?"

"I…I don't know," she replied, her body shaking.

"Let go of the Orb," I said calmly, taking a step towards her.

"I can't Clint," Caroline said, tears in her eyes. "It won't let me go. Please…someone help me."

Chapter 8

I felt a rising sense of panic running through my veins. Whatever I had just witnessed was like no magic I had yet experienced, and now I was unsure how to respond. Fortunately, at that moment, Selina burst into the room.

"I sensed dark magic," Selina said. "Are you all..." The words died on her lips as she caught sight of the Orb. "Damnit Clint, why did you let her pick up the Orb?"

"For one thing I had no idea where it was," I said, trying to remain calm in spite of the provocation. "Secondly, at that moment in time Niana's life was in imminent danger, I assumed that was a slightly higher priority in the grand scheme of things."

"Sorry," Selina said, sighing. "I just...if even half of what I've read about these things is true, its magic being released into the world is a VERY bad thing." She stepped in front of Caroline, looking her square in the eyes. "Caroline, do you trust me?"

"It...it hurts," Caroline replied, seeming at first to be unaware of Selina speaking to her, before blinking and looking at her again. "I...I need someone to help me."

"I know," Selina said, placing a hand on Caroline's shoulder. "This may feel a little…odd, but I promise it won't last long, okay?" Caroline nodded silently. For a moment Selina's hand glowed, and as she let go Caroline's eyes flickered shut, her body dropping to the floor as her grip on the Orb loosened, dropping it to the floor. "A sleep charm," Selina said. "A considerably less unpleasant version of the spell I used during our adventure at Fort Knox. Wait," she said, turning to spot I was about to pick the Orb up. "Nobody touches that, under any circumstances, till we're damn sure what it's capable of. Whether or not it helped you just now, anything that reeks of dark magic as much as that isn't going to do anything without a price."

"I heard a commotion from the other end of the corridor," Carlos said as he rushed into the room, stopping as he caught sight of the scene in front of him, visibly appearing to almost retch. "Why do I feel like I'm best off *not* asking what just happened in here?"

"We can explain," Selina replied. "But right now I need somewhere less claustrophobic to place Caroline while she recovers. I don't suppose there is a meeting room in this building?"

"There's a room the doctors use for their case reviews," Carlos answered. "Obviously it's not in use right now, it's not too far from here."

"Great," Selina said, turning to face me and Niana. "Carlos and I can make sure the Orb and Caroline make it to the room safely, you'd better radio the others and tell them to meet us there."

• • •

In a bit over five minutes everyone had regrouped in the home's recreation room, a room full of scattered puzzles all over the floor, the only other obvious features of the room a projector hanging from the ceiling and a cluster of filing cabinets at one end of the room. Carlos had placed the prone form of Caroline on a couch in the corner of the room, the Orb placed nearby. Selina was stood by the window, pacing back and forth, making sure we were brought up to speed with what had happened in the store room as rapidly as possible.

"They're all gone," Carlos said, grimacing. "Either they fled or that orb..." He paused, rubbing his eyes. "The hell kind of magic *is* that?"

"We've faced dark magic before," Mickey said. "We faced the damn God of Death, so how did this manage to catch us off guard?"

"What Feth'rael wielded was not necessarily dark magic," Selina replied. "Any magic can be set to an evil purpose in the wrong hands, but what that Orb contains is, unmistakably, dark magic."

"It's my fault," Carlos said despondently, slumping against a wall. "If I'd just insisted Caroline go with the others she wouldn't be—"

"Caroline will be fine," Selina said, trying to sound reassuring. "All I gave her was the magical equivalent of a very short-lived anaesthetic, she'll wake up soon enough." She walked over to one of the windows that looked onto the ground, indicating for me to join her. "We have a problem Clint," she said quietly, once I had joined her. "I'm not claiming to be an expert on those Orbs, but what I do know of them…literally sucking the souls out of something in their vicinity isn't any kind of spell I've come across."

"Are you saying you've researched dark magic?" I asked, raising an eyebrow more in amusement than accusation.

"That's not…" they said, stopping to let out a sigh. "Okay, I walked into *that* comment, I deserved it."

"There's one thing I don't get," I said, stealing a glance in the direction of the still body on the table. "You said she hasn't got a magical aura like a fairy would, how the hell did she manage to activate that weapon?"

"I don't know," Selina said, the concern written clearly across her face. "Either we're missing something here, or things are worse than we had imagined. If these things can be activated so easily then—"

"Then we've got weapons which could be triggered by near enough everyone," I interrupted, his face turning as white as a sheet. "How dangerous are they exactly?"

"That is difficult to estimate," Arkelion replied, appearing suddenly in the midst of the room. "Apologies for the surprise arrival, but the Orb activating triggered a response in the one in my possession."

"Who the hell are *you*?" Carlos asked, pulling his gun out, only to find Petra pushing his arm down. "Friend of yours I take it?"

"He is the mentor of Merzel and I," Petra replied. "He is no danger to you Carlos, he is here to help." I could see that, even as he holstered his gun, Carlos seemed unsure if he was doing the right thing. Petra turned to face Arkelion. "This human girl managed to wield its magics, I thought that was impossible?"

"It should be," Arkelion replied, leaning over Caroline. "The last human to wield magic this potent was—"

"She's not like him," Merzel said loudly, seeming to surprise even Arkelion. "She led Clint and the others to the Orb, so the idea that a large number of teenage humans were wandering around wielding some of the darkest magic known to—"

"Calm yourself young one," Arkelion said, raising a hand to stop him. "I did not mean to accuse her of any wrongdoing, it was merely an observation on my part."

"We need to locate the other Orbs," I said. "The next time one of these goes off we can't guarantee it won't be in a packed civilian area."

"I know where we can do that," Caroline said, sitting up suddenly. Fortunately, Arkelion had moved aside already so there was no danger of the two colliding. "There is a tree said to exist within Central Park, it's...I don't know why, but one of the other patients said it was called The Timeless Oak."

"My god, it can't be," Selina said quietly enough that only I, stood not far from them, could hear what she uttered.

"What are you talking about?" I asked, turning to find her cheeks flushed pink. "You've heard of this oak before, haven't you?"

"It's a legend," Selina answered. "At least...prior to just now I *assumed* that was what the Timeless Oak was. My mother told me of a nexus of fairy magic which was said to be capable of showing you whatever you wished, including the past and future. But she said it couldn't be true because no fairy, living or dead, has controlled magic on that scale before."

"That…is not entirely true," Arkelion replied. "There are two who have done so, one was the dark fairy who nearly toppled Europe, it was how he knew the attack was coming…as much use as that ultimately was to his cause. The other was in the great city of Glasswater, it is said that the book detailing how that spell could be cast was held somewhere within its walls."

"Guys," Selina said, biting their lip. "We…we have a problem. The library I spent time in as a kid was supposed to contain a copy of pretty much any fairy book short of the worst of the dark magic, I used to ask the librarian if there was a copy of my mother's story, she said that no-one would write such a story because it was absurd. But even then, with relatively underdeveloped magical powers, I could tell she was not being honest with me. So the only place this could book could possibly be is—"

"Glasswater," I interrupted, feeling my heart sink. "I get the distinct feeling someone, or something, wants us to go there, and my instincts say that can't mean anything good."

"Whether or not it is, you must go," Arkelion said. "The longer we worry about dangers which may never come to pass, the more chance there is that someone with less pure intentions will find their way into the Spire, then this will all become trivial."

"He's right everyone," Petra said. "We can take Carlos to where the patients are hiding and pick up Marek, but once that is done, we should head straight for the city." She turned to Arkelion. "Will you come with us?"

"I will accompany you to the patients," Arkelion replied. "But from there I should keep an eye on the Orbs. They may offer more clues, if only as to the location of the others." He held up a hand as Selina began a spell. "I will teleport us, the journey to Glasswater will be tiring enough without using your powers unnecessarily before then."

There was a brief flash of light, and once it had passed the room was emptied of everyone, and the Drakonite Orb. However, sat outside on the windowsill was a raven, staring at the place the group had been standing before. It launched into the sky, only one thought in its mind, that it had a long journey ahead of it.

Back in Las Vegas, in the corner of the casino where most of the patrons wouldn't dare set foot, Anera was in trouble. At that moment a tall, green-skinned brute had her pinned to a chair, a small silver knife held against her throat, while a short but stout goblin watched from a distance, an ill-fitting suit barely containing his frame, a pair of glasses perched on his nose, and a clipboard in his hand that he drummed impatiently every few minutes.

"We know they talked to you," the goblin snarled in a thick Texan accent. "Cut the crap and just tell us, and I'll tell Mag'ar here to make your death nice and quick."

"I'm dying anyway," Anera said, laughing and spitting in the goblin's direction. "You'll never find out where they're going, not from *me* anyway."

"I believe I can help you," came a voice from the

doorway, her guard stepping into the room. "She's too stubborn to tell you, but they're going to Glasswater, I can even show you how to get there."

"Why Tiberon?" Anera asked, tears in her eyes. "Why would you betray what we stand for after all these years by my side?"

"Because the Bloodfire Cartel offered one thing *you* never did," Tiberon snarled in response. "Pay, a future as something other than a bodyguard to a dying, forgetful old woman." He turned back to the goblin. "What do you say Gally, do we have a deal?"

For a moment Gally made no response, seeming to focus his gaze on a point over Tiberon's shoulder before looking at him.

"It's a deal," he replied, shaking Tiberon's hand, before nodding to the brute, who cut Anera's throat without a moment's pause. "Meet us outside Tiberon, we shall make sure this…unpleasantness is cleaned up as quietly as possible." Gally watched, Tiberion bowed and headed back the way he had come, before turning back to where he had been looking before, a smile crossing his face. "Did I do well mistress? Did we get what you wanted?"

"Oh, you did so much more than that Gally," came a female voice, as a tall, slender woman stepped from the shadows. She was dressed in a flowing blue dress, a pair of piercing red eyes shining from a pale face over which hung green hair, a pair of pointy ears just visible at either side of her head. "Gather your men and take them to Glasswater." Sensing the fear in the goblin she walked over, stroking his face gently. "Never fear my love, I will not be far behind, it is time the great dragon rose again."

Chapter 9

We got the Orb to Arkelion as soon as we were certain that the patients were safe. We all agreed that it was safer to leave it with someone who had some understanding as to how it worked than to risk running around with it ourselves. Then we teleported to Lake Wolff. The moment we rematerialized I couldn't help letting out a gasp as I took in our surroundings, the images I had seen barely began to do the location true justice. A mountain rose above a forest which covered almost the entirety of the opposite shore, only a small stretch of beach just visible from where I was stood. The majesty of the place had distracted me sufficiently that I was only released from the trance by a shout from Marek.

"Guys…I think you'd better see this," he said, a nervous tone to his voice. I turned to find a pick-up truck parked not far from the near bank of the lake. Selina, Niana and I all walked over. "I don't think it belongs to the nearby farmhouse," Marek said. "Even at this distance it doesn't take a genius to spot no-one's been in the place for several months. Could this be some kind of camping trip?"

"I don't think so," Selina said as she walked around the truck. "I don't see any kind of campsite nearby, besides most of what you'd want to do in this neck of the wood would be on the *other* side of the lake. It doesn't make sense, unless...oh no..."

"What is it?" Mickey asked, walking over to us.

"This place isn't really known for its tourism," Selina replied. "The most famous thing about it is it's a hotspot for hunters. They must have come here to shoot something, but all the animals are in that forest." They shivered slightly, leaning against Mickey as he came over and pulled them into a hug. "Sorry baby, I just have a particular hatred for people who shoot defenceless animals."

"Where is the city though?" Niana asked, looking around, frowning. "There should be *something* here if this was the location of America's biggest fairy city."

"Oh, you don't think your race know all the tricks, do you?" Petra asked, raising an eyebrow. "It wouldn't take that much effort to hide a city here if the person casting the spell had enough skill. There's every chance we might not spot the city until we were practically on top of it."

"Would a massive quantity of magic be a giveaway?" Crystal called from a short distance away. "Because I'm sensing it from what appears, to me, to just be a patch of long grass."

"That sounds about right," Petra said as I walked towards where Crystal was stood, the rest following closely behind. "There is a definite concentration of magic around here," Petra said, taking a few steps ahead of us, her hand moving to the short blade at her hip. I could feel it too, it was as if something was crawling all over my skin.

"Something's wrong, we need to be careful as we proceed. I'm getting a very bad feeling radiating from something close to us."

We stepped forward, the grass becoming so tall around us that soon I could no longer see my legs below the knee. I was about to comment on how strange this was when, in a change so quick it felt almost instantaneous, I found myself lying flat on the floor, the same stalks of grass towering high above us and letting through only the smallest slivers of light.

"You'd think I'd be used to that by now," I said, grunting as Niana gently helped me back to my feet.

"If it's any consolation, I'm not used to it," Niana said, kissing my cheek lightly. "And I've spent my whole life around magic like this. It does seem a little more...sudden than I remember though."

"Remember, this place dabbled in magic few other places did," Merzel said. "Don't assume everything will be familiar, we have to be o—"

His speech was cut short by a scream from nearby, which I instantly recognised as Selina's. Although we all moved towards where the noise came from at the same moment, my wings must have unfolded without me realising as I landed next to her, the question I wanted to ask dying on my lips as I saw what she had reacted to: she was stood in a nearby clearing in the grass, scattered around which were three men, which even the most cursory of glances made clear had been dead for some time, although no cause of said death was immediately obvious.

"I don't think we need to ask where the owner of that truck ended up," Crystal said, walking over to one man lying on his stomach, a pool of blood just visible around the body, as Mickey held a sobbing Selina close to him. "I hate people who hunt animals for sport as much as the next person," she continued, nodding to a gun which lay on the ground close to another man, who seemed to have been impaled on one of the stalks. "But this…it's like someone wanted to make an example of them. Who in god's name would be this brutal?"

"I'm not sure I can answer who," Petra replied. "But I have a feeling I can tell you where they came from."

We all followed the direction Petra was pointing, spotting something I was astounded we had missed when first entering the clearing. Where I would have expected to see more grass there was instead an imposing looking metal gate, the immense walls it formed part of spreading out and vanishing out of sight.

"Well, I guess that saves us having to look for Glasswater at least," Petra said, although the relief I would have expected to hear was notably absent from her voice. "But I really hope this wasn't intended as a 'Keep Out' warning, because I've gotta be honest if we didn't need to enter the city for help finding the orbs then I'd suggest we turn back and get as far away from Lake Wolff as we can. Merzel, can you sense anybody nearby?"

"There's too much magic shrouding the city," Merzel replied. "It could be empty, it could contain hundreds of thousands of fairies: without entering it I can't give you a definitive answer to the question."

"Let's be careful," Niana said, starting to walk towards the gate. "If these hunters were killed by the city's occupants, we don't want them considering us their enemy, not if we can avoid it anyway."

"And you think they're more likely to welcome you?" Petra asked.

"Well, I'm the only one here who belongs to a fairy royal family," Niana replied, now near enough to the gate that she seemed to vanish into a shadow I could've sworn moments before was not there. "There's more chance they'll listen to me than just a random visitor."

"Just…just be careful," I said, unable to shake the feeling something wasn't right, but not moving towards her. "We still don't know what's going on here."

"I'm not my brother Clint," Niana called out, chuckling loudly. "I do have *some* diplomatic talents." When she knocked on the gate the noise seemed to reverberate around the entire clearing, but nothing else happened. "Well, I should've guessed nothing was going to be *that* simple," she said, her footsteps beginning to return towards us. However, just as she appeared from out of the shadow my eyes were drawn back towards the gate.

Lines of a substance that appeared akin to liquid silver were slowly spreading across the door, giving the whole clearing an eerie glow.

"That's a pretty locking mechanism," Mickey said.

"It's no locking mechanism," Petra said. "We've made a massive mistake, we're—"

I didn't hear the rest of Petra's advice, as a burst of silver light exploded outwards from the gate, forcing me to lose consciousness before I hit the ground.

At first, I could hear two voices speaking, which made me wonder if I'd fallen asleep and everything had been a strange dream, until the pain of hitting the ground hit me with a throbbing sensation. I tried to focus on the voices, and realised neither was a voice I recognised. One was a male voice which sounded low and gruff, while the other was a woman's, but it sounded distant, as if hearing it through an especially distant phone receiver. I slowly opened my eyes, my first sight that of Niana's unconscious form lying to my left, thankfully no sign of a bad injury immediately obvious.

What caught my attention more was what was happening around us: a strange green light was flowing around us, occasionally going through our clothes before emerging again. All I could tell for certain was that my pain seemed to be slowly diminishing.

"This is the garden of El'Thalel," came the man's voice, which made me sit up just enough to locate the source, getting my first look at where we were.

It was a circular courtyard, surrounded by tall trees, at the centre of which was a large fountain from which poured crystal clear water. Stood next to it was a tall male fairy, dressed in robes which were a shade of dark red, with a turquoise cape draped over his shoulder, beneath which I caught a glint of a pair of silver daggers. His face, framed by short blue hair, was such a mix of worry lines and scars his yellow eyes were almost impossible to spot.

Stood next to him was an older female fairy, dressed in plain white robes, but after a moment I realised there was something odd about her appearance. I could see the fountain through her, as if she was a hologram, or…

"My apologies for the events at the gate," the male fairy said, sighing. "I forgot this place has certain…defence mechanisms to stop unwanted visitors."

"You mean like those men outside?" I asked, the image of the bodies coming to the front of my mind. "Why did we live and yet they were slaughtered?"

"You do not know the story of what happened here," the male fairy replied, his hand moving to one of the daggers. "You all left—"

"Son," the female fairy said sharply. "They did *nothing*, they are only children." She turned to look at me, a faint smile playing across her lips. "I am glad to see the magic worked quickly." I looked around, noticing the others were either already awake, or in the case of Niana were slowly regaining consciousness. I pulled her into a hug, which after a few moments she returned. "You must excuse my son, he has seen horrors I would not wish on anyone."

"This is Glasswater, isn't it?" Petra asked, looking around. "Or at least, part of it anyway."

"This is…" the woman started saying, before frowning. "This *was* the site of the royal palace, before it happened." She paused for a moment. "My name is Princess Delarein, once the second in line to this throne. This fine specimen is my son, Crown Prince Arkon, one of Glasswater's greatest soldiers, and now its last living resident."

"Last living..." I stopped, the woman's strange appearance finally making sense to me. "You're a ghost, aren't you?" Delarein nodded. "What happened here? We could find only one book that referred to your city, and that one gave only scant detail."

"See, I told you, they forgot about us," Akerion snarled. "We sold our lives to protect them and *this* is what we get in return?"

"A...friend of ours said an attempt to erase all your records wouldn't result in this," Selina replied. "Why, if you could erase all records of this city, would you leave a way to trace it?"

"You said you were protecting us," Niana said. "What were you protecting us from?"

"Akerion, get our guests food," Delarein said, keen to avoid further confrontation. "I assume you know the reputation Glasswater gained for the magics practiced here?" she asked, once her son had vanished through one of the archways. We nodded in response. "What few realized, what few *still* realize, is what directly influenced it."

"The stories of this place being a hub for dark magic were true then?" I asked.

"It is worse than that," Delarein responded. "There is a chamber beneath this city that contains something whose true danger we only discovered when it was too late to reverse the devastation it created."

"You're already telling them about the Vault of Eternity?" Akerion asked as he returned, a table covered in bread and fruit floating a short distance behind him. "You used to tell me even our great guardians were not allowed to know of its existence."

"That was before it destroyed this city my child," the ghost replied. "The magic coming from it is only getting stronger, the runes that enclose this city cannot last forever, their arrival here may be most fortunate timing."

"This vault, it contains an orb, doesn't it?" I asked, my blood running cold as Delarein nodded. "Shit, I was hoping you wouldn't say that."

"How would that be possible?" Mickey asked. "How would a Drakonite Orb get here? I can't imagine there were soldiers of Glasswater there when the battle was fought."

"There wouldn't need to be," Selina replied. "Mickey darling, we only know the location of two of the orbs, and we only have hearsay for the fact a third is lost at the bottom of the ocean." They were silent for a few moments. "Delarein, we need to know everything you can possibly tell us about the vault, its contents and as much detail about what happened to this place as you can tell us."

"What about the book?" Crystal asked. "We're here for that, at least I *thought* that was why we were here."

"We saw what the Drakonite weapons could do on a small scale at the hospital," Selina answered. "If one of them destroyed a city and is only getting *more* powerful, it is our priority, whether it was our original intention or not."

"You had best come to the library," Akerion said. "If you're going to discover the full story of what happened here...you're going to want to be sitting down."

• • •

The library wasn't all that far from the garden we had woken up in, set in a large one-storey building which was in the midst of an area which seemed surrounded by the skeletal remains of trees. Niana's grip on my hand tightened, only relaxing slightly as we entered the building. It was full of shelves packed to the brim with books, scrolls and even the occasional glass container holding strange artefacts. Akerion waved his hand, a set of elaborate wooden armchairs appearing out of the floor. We took our seats as he walked towards one of the shelves, leaving his mother to turn to face us.

"Glasswater has been here, to the best of my knowledge, for at least six hundred years," she said, once the room had fallen silent. "But the location we know as the Vault of Eternity was here before the city was founded. Indeed our historians suspected it may have been part of a previous city. But as the city was built around it the decision was made to not attempt to open its sealed door."

"Why not?" I asked. "Admittedly I've not seen it for myself, but wouldn't a mystery like that pique most people's curiosity?"

"It seems even then they knew something was wrong," Akerion replied, returning with a large, cloth-bound book. "The old stories talk of a strange aura that surrounded it, which led them to forming a group of magically skilled guards. Their job was to both stop people entering the vault and to avoid the potential for something to escape it and threaten the city. But then the dark magic users suddenly emerged. For a century it was only a handful of such fairies, but the frequency increased, making it more difficult for the royal family and the ruling council to either try and cover it up or ignore the likelihood something else was at work. When they finally found one of the dark magic users who was willing and able to speak to them, that's when they found out about the voices people were hearing."

"Hearing voices? That's what sca..." Marek's comment, and a deep chuckle, ended as soon as I gave him a harsh glare, which caused him to shrink back into his chair.

"What were the voices saying?" Selina asked.

"No-one seemed entirely certain," Delarein replied. "To complicate things further, the few people who *could* understand what they were hearing described different sentences. Some claimed they heard the voice of a dead relative, others said it was chanting in a language they couldn't make sense of, but most could handle the effects, and those that couldn't were exiled to avoid any long-term effects on the city's morale."

"I think I know what happened," Selina said. "We still don't completely understand how these things work, but…This might seem like an odd question, but did it get worse the more people there were who displayed their abilities?"

"I can only go off the records and speak of what happened within my lifetime," Delarein answered. "But yes, from what I can tell the problem became progressively worse. Why do you ask?"

"I think I know what caused it," Selina said, resting their head in their hands. "Not for certain, but I have a suspicion. The only orb we've seen in action fed off people's life force. What if one of them fed off magic? It could become a vicious circle, the more powerful it becomes the more magic it hungers for—"

"And the more dark magic spreads through the city," I said, finishing her sentence. "But if that's true then what devastated the city like this?"

"It began four years ago," Akerion replied. "There hadn't been someone punished for using dark magic within the boundaries of this city for 40 years, there was relative peace for once. But then a child who walked near to the vault claimed to have heard voices again, except now the message was audible to anyone."

"'Leave this city or I will feed on your magic until your vault cannot contain me'", Delarein said. "It took all my mother's skill to calm the child to the point where he no longer had nightmares about what he had heard. As far as Glasswater's populace were aware the Vault, and several streets around it, were considered off limits to all comers. But a special selection of guards was placed around it, while the greatest magic users in the city began a desperate search for an explanation and, if possible, a solution."

"But it was too late," Selina said quietly. "It was spreading dark magic again, wasn't it? That's why the voice started again."

"At first it was manageable," Akerion replied. "But then 2 years ago it became impossible to hide what was happening. Dark magic was emerging seemingly unbidden, by the time we realised the full scale of what was transpiring we couldn't tackle it alone."

"And we could not risk asking others for help,"

Delarein said, nodding. "If we couldn't be sure what the cause was, we ran the risk that the problem would spread outside our borders and infect other cities."

"Two years..." Crystal said, before letting out a groan. "The night all the kids reported the same sighting, I don't like coincidences at the best of times, but these have got to be linked in some way."

"I think it might be worse than that," Selina said. "The disaster, the one that destroyed the city, it happened a year ago, didn't it? It's why Akerion is the only sign of life here." There was an uncomfortable silence, before Akerion nodded. "The war with Feth'rael, it may not have triggered the Orb waking up again, but it triggered something within it."

"Are you saying the Death God *chose* to destroy this city?" Akerion asked incredulously.

"If he'd meant to do this, he wouldn't have been able to keep his mouth shut," Selina replied. "But the amount of dark magic in the world, especially around his ritual...it wouldn't have taken much to give this thing the nudge required."

"I thought we were saving people," I said, staring at the floor. "We killed more people than we could begin to realise."

"It is not your fault," Delarein said. "You could not have known what was transpiring here, an army could not have reversed the devastation that occurred. It was..." She paused. "I will spare you the details of what occurred, but when my son returned from aiding the battle against Feth'rael, there were no survivors."

"I'm not sure that's entirely true," Nara, who had been sat next to Crystal in silence, said. "A young woman arrived at the gates of Niana's home city carrying a child with the birthmark of your city a short time ago. We could take you to meet them…if you wish."

"That is something Akelion can do once this situation is dealt with," Delarein said. "But for now we must tackle the more urgent task. We cannot allow this…orb you mention to remain here any longer, we will show you where the vault is, and then I can explain the way we can gain access to it safely."

We were led back through the garden, passing through between ruined buildings, not stopping until we reached a large open space, dominated by what, at first, I assumed was an empty fountain. It was only as we got closer I realised it was an immense circular cover, upon which was inscribed a series of strange runes. I couldn't help noticing a sense of unease hanging in the air around us.

"Selina and I can work on the seals of the vault," Delarein said. "I advise you all make yourselves comfortable, I am unsure how much time this will take to complete."

As the rest of us spread out I walked towards the edge of the courtyard, in the direction I guessed Lake Wolff would be relative to my current position. I was so deep in thought I didn't realize I had company until I felt Niana's hand slip gently into mine.

"A penny for your thoughts hun?" she asked, lifting my hand so she could kiss the knuckles.

"I just..." I paused, shivering slightly. "I feel like we should've done something, like we could've spared this city. Imagine what this place would've been like back then."

"You can't think that," Niana said. "We had no idea what was happening, none of us did. And even if we had...magic capable of destruction like this, you wouldn't have been able to stop it back then. We'll find a way to stop this happening again, okay?"

"Okay," I said, kissing her cheek. "You always know the right thing to say, I wish—" My words were cut off by an ear-splitting scream from the direction we'd come from, one I recognised immediately. "Marek," I said, turning around to face the others.

"I will keep Selina safe," Akerion said. "You make sure the child is safe."

We required no further encouragement, running back to the healing courtyard, where we found Marek with his back to us, pointing at the sky.

"We...we have a problem guys," he said after a moment.

"I don't...see..." I started saying, until I caught sight of the dark shape emerging from the glare of the Sun. "Oh god...someone tell me that's a bird, or even an airplane."

"That's a dragon," Petra said, sounding panicked.

"I thought dragons were a myth?" Marek asked. "I've only seen them in kids' stories."

"Well, considering we're in the middle of a ruined city?" Niana asked. "We sure as hell better *hope* they're a myth."

Chapter 10

For a few moments, we were stood in stunned silence, only broken when we realised the dragon was approaching the city rapidly.

"We need to warn the others," Petra said. "Dragons don't start flying in broad daylight to make social calls. And, I hate to point this out, but…that thing looks a *lot* like the dragon from outside the casino."

"I thought that thing was fake?" Mickey said as we hurried back to the vault. "For a statue it seems to be very real."

"In fairness you'd think a real dragon in the middle of Las Vegas would stick out like a sore thumb," Petra replied as we reached the vault. "But I don't believe this is the work of a fairy, whatever this is has magic I'm not familiar with."

"There's a dragon coming?" Selina asked, my attention suddenly drawn to the bubble of transparent grey magic that surrounded her. "Ordinarily I would consider that possibly the coolest thing I've ever heard about, but I need to not be distracted right about now."

"I can help you," Akerion said, turning to the rest of us.

"No offence to any of you but I suspect I have more experience of fighting in a direct battle, but someone will have to stay here, in case something happens."

"Marek," I volunteered, turning as I heard the growl of annoyance he uttered. "Marek, you went toe to toe with a god of death and walked away again, if keeping watch on this vault is beyond your abilities, I doubt any of us will fare any better."

"You know I'm going to get you back for this one day, right?" Marek asked, letting out a resigned sigh.

"I'm sure you will," I replied, trying, and failing, to suppress a laugh, not helped by the fact Niana was laughing. "But for now we have bigger fish...or should I say dragons...to fry."

I breathed a sigh of relief that, rather than having to make our way through the grim remains of the city, Akerion teleported us to just outside the gate, bringing us back to full size just in time for us to catch our first full sight of the approaching beast. In full flight its wings would have put even the largest jet airliner to shame, its scales ice blue, and as it got closer, we finally got a glimpse of its rider. They were dressed in a dark blue cloak that was pulled so close all that could be glimpsed was a sliver of a grey tunic beneath and a pair of armoured gauntlets that gripped a set of reins. The dragon landed more deftly than I would have expected it to, its amber eyes focusing on us as the rider slid off its back, even a quick glimpse revealing they were taller than even Akerion, who was easily the tallest of our group.

"I am Akerion, protector of this land," Akerion said calmly, although I couldn't help noticing his hand lingering near where I suspected his daggers were on his belt. "There has not been a dragon rider here since the days of my ancestors, what brings you to my domain?"

"Your friends have something I wish to…acquire," the rider replied, before chuckling. "My apologies, it is rude of me to not introduce myself properly." The gauntlets moved the hood aside, revealing a pale face with silver eyes, long red hair and ears that elicited a gasp from most of our group.

"Clint," Mickey, who was stood next to me uttered, "she's…she's a—"

"Yes, I'm an elf," the woman said, laughing. "I should have guessed my fae cousins would not have exposed you to our kind, they have considered us elves as the black sheep of the magical family for as long as human civilization has existed."

"Cut the crap elf," Niana said through gritted teeth. "You didn't fly a dragon all the way here for a family reunion, who are you and what do you want?"

"I see you are not one for small talk," the elf replied, the smile on her face vanishing. "My name is Car'aelan, I am a…representative of a group who call ourselves the Bloodfire Cartel. We know you possess some of the last relics of the Drakonite civilization, I'm here to take them off your hands and return them to their rightful owners."

"Even if we had one, like hell would we hand it to you," Petra growled. "You have no damn idea the magic you're dealing with, I'm certainly not handing it to a group I didn't know existed till just now. So go back to Vegas and pick a fight with someone else."

"You children are so tiresome," Car'aelan said, stepping forward, moving her cloak enough to show a large broadsword at her belt. "Allow me to be clearer: I *will* be leaving with the orb you are hiding, it is up to you whether I permit you to escape this place alive."

"I get the dragon is impressive and all," Merzel said, scoffing. "But considering it only counts as one creature you're still outnumbered, what exactly is your plan here?"

"How cute you think I'd turn up alone," the elf said, letting out a low whistle. Within a moment we found ourselves surrounded by goblins, most armed with short but vicious looking blades. But the biggest surprise was saved for last: Tiberon, Anera's guard, stepped up beside the elf.

"Why would…" Petra started saying, before she let out a gasp. "Why? She trusted you, and *this* is how you repay her?"

"I was wasted with her," Tiberon replied. "She wanted me to protect her library, I would've died of boredom long before anyone wanted to steal from her. The Cartel offered me the chance to gain real power, the kind no forgotten *Sidhe* could possibly provide."

"If you had any idea what magic you were dealing with you wouldn't even *consider* helping them," Akerion said. "This is no children's parlour trick you are meddling with, people *will* die if you misuse this power. An entire city already *has* died."

"Evidently these idiots aren't smart enough to do as

they're told," Car'aelan said, sighing. "I guess we'll have to do this the old-fashioned way then."

With that, and after a few moments where time itself seemed to stop, all hell broke loose. The goblins charged straight at us, giving us barely enough time to form a makeshift defensive line, my own sword only just drawn quickly enough to block a wickedly sharp blade aimed at my neck. I let out a small sigh of relief as I realized, although not by design, that I had ended up closest to Niana, who fought with a ferocity that those who had never spent time with her might assume a small, relatively fragile-looking young woman was incapable of producing. To my other side Merzel was wielding a pair of short blades as easily as most people would their dinner cutlery. I was so caught by his balletic manoeuvres that I only avoided a stab to the leg because Niana drove her blade up through the goblin's gut, pulling it out.

"Clint, when I said yes, I kind of hoped you'd stay alive long enough for us to actually get married," she said, looking at me as she attempted to suppress a laugh. "Can you try not to get distracted when an army is trying to kill us?"

"Just be glad the dragon isn't getting involved," Merzel said, taking a moment to wipe a drop of blood off one of his blades. "My grandfather told me tales of the old dragon hunters of North America: they became legends because very few lived to tell their tale, and even then, it was more often due to the dragon getting bored and letting them escape."

Before I could respond I felt a ripple pass around me, turning to find Akelion had cast some form of spell which, while not eliminating the entire threat, had succeeded in knocking those goblins nearest to us off their feet. I only had enough time to give him a brief nod of thanks before more goblins reached us, the sound of the battle around me blocking out any of the sounds of nature I had heard when we first appeared in the area. I became so numb to the events around me I was only distracted from the back and forth of the battle by the sound of a voice in my head.

"Clint, we have a problem," Crystal's voice said, as clearly as if she had been stood right next to me. "Have you noticed who's missing from this attack?"

At first, I couldn't figure out what she meant, until a glance to my right made it obvious: while the vast, if currently motionless, form of the dragon was still visible neither the elf, nor Tiberon, were anywhere to be seen.

"Akelion," I called out, forced to give the majority of my attention to the battle around me. "Why do I get the awful feeling this attack wasn't their real plan at all?"

"The city," Akelion said. "They know, with the rest of my kind gone, I'm one of the only things maintaining the city's defences, if I'm out here fighting…" He made a loud exclamation in a language I couldn't even begin to understand. "Petra, Clint, with me, the Vault is in danger."

"And the rest of us are doing *what* exactly?" Merzel asked.

"Keep these goblins occupied," Niana replied, pulling me into a kiss before pushing me towards Akelion. "Whether or not this is intended as a distraction, the last thing they need is getting trapped between an army and a potentially dangerous elf. Just make sure you're still in one piece when I next see you," she said to me, smiling as I felt the world around me twist, the battle vanishing before my eyes.

Although it was a matter of seconds before we materialized, it felt as if several minutes had passed, although I was glad that the momentary sensation of my body twisting was only fleeting. My impression of a prolonged experience was not helped by the fact the scene around the vault had changed. The stone covering that had kept it covered had been smashed into pieces, which lay all around the large hole which now dominated our surroundings. To one side was Selina, lying on their back, a small cut on their right cheek, but otherwise seemingly unharmed.

"Marek," they said as we approached. "The elf took Marek with her into the Vault."

"How did she do that?" I asked as Petra took a closer look at Selina's injury. "Not even telekinesis could do that to a structure that solidly built."

"My vision was too foggy at that point to get a proper look," Selina replied. "But there is something…wrong about her magical aura, if you're going to confront her you need to be careful." They gently pushed Petra's hand away. "I've recovered from worse, your priority needs to be the Orb, go give her an extra hard smack from me, will you?"

"We'll do our best," I replied, laughing for a moment before realising the others were about to jump into the hole, forcing me to fly a short distance to keep up with them. When we dived inside it took about a minute before we landed on a rocky floor. As I looked around, I initially thought my eyes were having to adjust to the darkness, but then realised there wasn't a lack of light, what looked like a black liquid was flowing around us in such quantity that I was struggling to catch more than a glimpse of the torches that lined the wall. "So...I'm pretty sure this isn't natural...I'm right, aren't I?"

"It's dark magic," Akelion replied. "If it builds up enough it can develop a life of its own. I...I know that's hard to get your head around, but magic doesn't always work the way you wish it to. If this is right...this amount of magic should have burst out repeatedly, this artifact you're looking for is choosing when to be active and when to be dormant."

"Sentient magical weapons?" Petra asked. "Great, because thirteen potentially lethal spells in close proximity to untrained teenagers wasn't a worrying scenario by itself." While she was talking, she had begun to walk further into the Vault, but came to a sudden halt. "We have company," she said quietly, pointing further into the vault. A small pool of light illuminated the forms of Car'aelan and Tiberon, even before we could hear their speech it was clear they were in the midst of a heated discussion.

"I promised you help," Tiberon said angrily. "But this...this is no relic, this would be considered a weapon of mass destruction if a human built it."

"I did not bring you here to assuage your guilty conscience fool," Car said. "Help me or don't, the Cartel is only interested in gaining possession of the contents of that artefact."

"You'll have to go through me first," Tiberon said,

drawing his sword. "My old mistress may have been a fool but at least she wasn't playing with magic she barely understood."

"I was trained by one of the greatest swordsmen to ever live," Car said, drawing her own broadsword. "If you think I'm scared of you then *you* are the fool." There was a sudden sound from our direction, and when she spotted us, she laughed. "Oh, we have an audience, this'll be fun."

"You're outnumbered, elf," Petra spat. "Get the hell out of this city and we might just allow you to walk away with your life."

"I don't need a sword to beat children like you," Car snarled. "You weren't even a glint in your parents' eyes when I learnt how to use mag—" She yelped suddenly, all of us suddenly seeing a bloodied, but determined-looking, Marek had plunged a dagger into her foot, breaking her concentration. "You brat, I'll kill you for that."

"Not today," Tiberon growled, bringing his sword up to block the swing aimed at Marek's unprotected right arm. "This may not make up for what I did to Anera, but it is at least a start."

"I've wasted enough time in this hellhole already," Car said, stepping back. "However, I can at least…repay you for your change of heart Tiberon," she said, pulling something from under her cloak that Petra and I recognised instantly.

"Petra, that's—"

"A Drakonite Orb," Petra said as we caught sight of the familiar shape. "How the hell do you have one of those?"

"That's for me to know and you never to discover," the

elf replied, eerie green light spreading out from the Orb. "Goodbye, I'm sure we'll meet again."

Before even Marek could make a move there was a sudden flash of light, and when it cleared the only sign that either elf or her former ally had been stood there was Marek's dagger, which fell harmlessly to the floor.

"That…that can't be the Orb from the hospital, can it?" I asked, feeling the colour drain from my face.

"No, it's worse," came Selina's voice from behind us. I turned to discover she was leaning against a wall of the cavern, breathing heavily. "Petra, I advise you call Arkelion and tell him to come here, he may need to know this."

"You sound like you know the spell," I asked Selina, as Petra walked to a more secluded part of the vault. "How is that possible?"

"I went through a phase where I was obsessed with learning about all forms of magic," she replied. "Despite my mother's repeated warnings, I insisted I wanted to know about dark magic, so she told me about one of the few forbidden spells whose name was known to all, believing it would dissuade me from investigating further. Its name is the Living Death."

"She killed Tiberon?" Marek asked. "After he helped her get here?"

"No, the Living Death is worse," Selina replied. "It doesn't kill its victims, it is used in combination with a magical artefact, the victims are trapped in said object alive, aware of everything that happens and in unimaginable pain, but incapable of freeing themselves." She slid to the floor.

"Crap, I should've known a group like the Drakoni would utilise a spell like that."

"But how would the Cartel get hold of the Orb?" Akelion asked. "I have heard stories that they hoard artefacts, but this lies outside their standard expertise."

For a few minutes we all either sat or stood in stunned silence, until Selina's phone suddenly rang. Having answered it, her face went white.

"Spyke," she said. "I'm putting you on speakerphone, tell everyone what you just told me."

"Hey everyone," Spyke said. "So, I've been looking into the files again, to see if I could garner any information I hadn't spotted before and…I've found something. It turns out one of the kids never made it to a hospital. I mean, he was supposed to, but the day they came to pick him up his parents found he'd run away. Three days later his dead body turned up, stabbed with a blade no pathologist could identify."

"Where did he come from?" I asked, feeling with a sense of dread that I knew what his answer would be.

"A little place in Nevada, just outside Las Vegas," Spyke replied. "Why? What's happened?"

"We need to go to Las Vegas," Petra replied. "Because otherwise that Orb is about to have one hell of a buffet."

Chapter 11

"I don't mean to sound like the pessimist in the room," Mickey said. "But even if we get lucky and the Cartel aren't expecting us, a group like that aren't going to be stupid enough to just leave the thing lying around where any Tom, Dick or Harry can stroll in and pick it up."

"He's right," Petra said. "And I doubt they would be hiding in the casino either. If we're going to pull this off, we're going to have to put a proper amount of thought into it."

"Maybe I can help," Arkelion said, suddenly appearing in our midst, so suddenly in fact I couldn't help noticing Selina's jumpy response. "My apologies, but locating one of the Orbs is certainly something that requires my immediate attention." He took a few steps towards the Orb, before visibly flinching and taking a step back. "This...I have seen many things in this world, but dark magic this strong, on this scale...this is something far more dangerous."

"Do you have somewhere it could be safely stored?" Selina asked. "If it's left here what happened in Glass-water...this could be the first of many disasters it causes."

"There is one place," Arkelion replied. "It is far enough away that I would suggest I take it there alone, you need to locate the others as rapidly as possible. I have finally identified the magic utilized by the orb I had when our groups first met. It is so rare that the name does not have an…easy name even for my tongue, but its effects involve what I believe humans would describe as 'mind control'."

"All we need now is a spell to rid people of emotion," Mickey said, letting out a light laugh. "That way they'd be every stereotypical movie bad gu—" He stopped talking as Selina nudged him none too gently in the ribs. "Okay, that sounded a lot funnier in my head, I swear."

"We have another problem," Petra said. "At least…it might be a problem. Arkelion, you told us when we were kids that humans were incapable of wielding magic?"

"That was what had been told to me," the aged fairy replied, looking around the group. "What has happened?"

"The girl back at the hospital," Petra replied. "The one who had the orb in her possession…She had magic skills most fairies would envy, how would that even be possible?"

"I'm not certain," Arkelion replied, although I looked in his direction long enough to notice there was more recognition in his eyes than he seemed to acknowledge. "That may imply more lives are at risk than we had originally assumed however." He suddenly flinched, turning towards the exit to the vault. "Children, there is someone else here, they are…definitely not a fairy."

"What odds one of our goblin friends decided to stick around?" I asked. "We shouldn't all go take a look, they've tricked us once."

"I'll go," Akerion said. "I know this place better than any of you do, plus if this is a trap, I'd rather we *didn't* all walk into an ambush at once."

Before any of us could attempt to argue with him he had vanished, returning moments later with a rather disheveled-looking goblin in a vice-like grip. Although I didn't recognise him from the battle outside the walls, the ragged blue uniform he wore was instantly recognisable as belonging to the casino we had visited.

"Our…'friend' here claims he's here to speak to you," Akerion said, causing me to step forward, only for Akerion to shake his head, pointing past me. I followed his gaze, realising it had settled on Crystal. "He asked for you directly by name."

"What could you possibly want with me?" Crystal asked, taking a tentative step forward.

"My name is Galleyria," the goblin replied. "Although most call me Gally. She called me Gally…" he said, pausing for a few moments. "I came here because of your friend Nara, they've…they've taken her."

"How would they capture Nara?" Mickey asked. "I thought she was visiting her mother back in Cornwall?"

"That's…not strictly true," Crystal replied. "I didn't tell you guys because at the time I assumed it wasn't relevant to what we were doing. She came to the US to trace a colony of exiled Pixies, to try and trace the origins of an old Pixie myth that no-one in Cornwall could explain. But…what would the Cartel want with her? Unless…" She paused, the colour seeming to drain from her face, before she drew her blade and took several steps towards Gally. "They need her to find something, don't they?"

"They can't locate the other orbs," Gally replied. "They assumed the one the elf carried could be used to track the rest of the dark magic, but it didn't work out like that. Then a…little birdie told them about your lady's special skills; kidnapping her was the obvious solution." He looked between each of the group in turn, a grin crossing his face. "*Damn*, you have no idea what I'm talking about do you? Too scared to let them know the truth, Crystal?"

"Crystal isn't—" I started to say, realising too late that she had vanished from the vault. "Keep an eye on him," I said through gritted teeth. "I'm going to go make sure Crystal is okay."

If you'd asked me, even in the immediate aftermath, how I'd known Crystal's location at that moment I would've struggled to explain. But somehow, I managed to teleport straight to her location. She was sat down, her back resting against the fountain that had been our first glimpse of the city, the faintest trail of tears visible on her face. Thinking better of trying to force her to talk I sat down next to her, placing my hand near enough to hers that it was there should she need it.

"Nara has an ability," Crystal said after a few moments of silence. "I don't know whether it's one all Pixies have, or whether it's unique to her. The short version of it? She can sense dark magic, not always the exact spell being used, but it would explain why the Cartel would abduct her."

"That's not what upset you though, is it?" I asked, wincing as I saw her clench her fists. "I didn't mean to make you angry."

"It's not you Clint," Crystal said. "I discovered Nara's powers because I have…been having nightmares. More vivid ones than I remember having at any other point in my life." She paused, taking a deep breath. "Clint, do you remember what Feth'rael said to us…to me in New York?"

"About you being his child?" I asked. "Oh Crystal, he probably said that just to taunt you, that can't possibly be true."

"That's the problem Clint," Crystal replied, turning to look at me. "I've been having nightmares about him since…since not long after the war ended. At first I thought it was nothing, but then Nara woke me up one night and revealed to me she had caught me chanting a spell in a language she didn't recognise. She didn't have to though, because she could sense the dark magic forming an aura around me."

For a few moments there was silence between us, as I struggled to make sense of what I had just been told.

"Clint…" Crystal finally said. "I'm…I'm scared I'm turning into him, that whatever is causing the sudden emergence of this magic will take control of me. I don't know what would happen if I lost control of it…I might be as much a threat to you as—"

"Crystal," I said softly, squeezing her hand. "Look, I can't pretend to know what the future will hold, but I refuse to believe you could ever turn into that kind of…monster.

You have empathy, you have love, you have morals… Feth'rael could only dream of possessing all of those."

"That's what Nara has been telling me," Crystal said, wiping her eyes. "If I didn't have you two to keep me sane during all of this, I don't know what I'd do." She stood up, taking a deep breath. "Come on, we have a goblin to finish interrogating, and right now I've got a strong desire to wipe that smug look off his face."

Our first priority once we had returned to the others was to fill them in on what Crystal had just told me, in order to avoid Gally making any further attempts to antagonise our group. Thankfully the response she received was supportive from everyone.

"Okay, cut the crap Gally," Crystal said, stepping in front of him. "Much as I…dislike the concept of helping you in any way, we can't get what we want without your help. So…consider this a temporary truce, and start talking."

"Shake on it?" Gally asked, offering his hand, although none of us took a single step closer to him. "Well, I can't say that especially surprises me." He sighed, waving a hand in the air, which caused a scroll to appear in front of him. As we all gathered around it I was surprised to discover the map seemed far larger than I had thought at first glance, images seeming to form on the paper even as we watched.

"Okay, I'm impressed," Mickey said. "I don't suppose you can teach me how to do that?"

"I'm not doing anything," Gally said, grunting. "This

paper came to me enchanted, it was intended to make it more difficult for people to find the secret entrance to the Cartel's base. Luckily for all of you, people are yet to invent a spell I can't find a way round." He pointed to a building at the centre of the map, whose shape was instantly familiar as that of the casino, before indicating what looked like tentacles snaking out around the building. "The Cabal's main security precaution," Gally continued. "Some of these lead to traps, some to dead ends, the middle of the Nevada desert...only one of these leads to Fort Dawnleer, the Cabal's secret headquarters. This one," he said, pointing to the northernmost passage.

"Great, he's shown us where to go," Marek said. "Remind me *why* we need him at all?"

"You think magical crooks are dumb enough to let people just walk in and out of their hideout at will?" Gally asked scornfully. "I thought you humans were supposed to be the *intelligent* ones on this planet."

"I think what our companion here meant to say," I said, sensing Mickey was about to fly into a rage, "was how he can help us bypass their security measures."

"There are only a handful of guards on that tunnel," Gally said. "Partly because they're cocky enough to believe most people won't locate it, but also because of the magic that lines it." He paused, closing his eyes as if mentally preparing himself for what came next. "Everyone thinks goblins don't have magic, but that's not true. We just don't possess offensive magic like most races. Our skills are more in the area of traps and illusions. So—"

"So if we try walking down that tunnel unprepared the

best case scenario is we get lost and never find our way out," Mickey said, groaning. "Yeah, point taken, I apologise for misjudging you Gally."

"In fairness I wouldn't trust me as far as I could throw me either," Gally said, chuckling. "The Cartel are gonna be smart enough to expect you though, if we're going, we'd better go now."

"We have questions that need answering," Petra replied. "Are we supposed to just ignore them?"

"I will be here when you return," Arkelion replied. "I feel this Orb is not safe to move until I have brought its magic under control. Simply return with it and then, I promise, I will give you what answers I can."

"I'll go ahead," Gally said, putting his hands up immediately "I'm not trying to pull anything, but my chances of helping you get into the fortress are severely hampered if I turn up with you guys, they'll never let either of us in that way. Give me five minutes, I promise you'll know where to go by then."

With that, and before any of us could attempt to make a protest, Gally vanished into thin air.

"Well, there's every chance we're walking straight into a trap," Merzel said. "I just hope we don't wind up regretting trusting the word of a mob boss."

"This is the one and only time I'm gonna say this brother," Petra said, a smirk playing across her lips. "If this does turn out to be an ambush, you have my permission to say 'I told you so'…and I can already tell I'm gonna regret that."

• • •

When the five minutes had passed Petra teleported us to the same location just across from the entrance of the casino that we had appeared at the first time we had been there. However, this time we were caught off-guard by the fact the Pixie guard who had been at the door previously was waiting for us this time.

"Gally told me you were coming," he said, putting his hands up in as non-threatening a way as possible. "I promise I'm on your side, but you can't just walk in the front door, the whole place is on edge. Besides, I may not have lived in Cornwall for several years, but Pixies are expected to do everything they can to protect each other. I don't care how much these pricks are paying me, I'm not letting them get away with kidnapping."

"Then what are you suggesting?" I asked, feeling a little cautious, in spite of his attempts at being friendly.

"A place like this, you can't afford people noticing potentially…shady activities such as entering and leaving the building, and especially not human law enforcement," the Pixie replied. "There are other ways into the building, you're going to have to trust me to teleport you there though."

"I don't think we have a choice," Selina said, before anyone else could comment. "Our friend…"

"Marean," the Pixie replied.

"Marean, is offering us as safe a way into the building as we're likely to get, unless any of you have a better idea?" They allowed us a few moments to see if anyone would protest, but they let out a chuckle when we responded with nothing more than a stony silence. "Come on then Marean, let's get a move on."

In the time it took me to suggest we should hold hands, I suddenly realised we were inside a room that seemed part basement, part cavern. I couldn't help feeling relief that the only people around me who didn't seem shocked at this turn of events were Marean and Selina, the latter seeming immensely amused by the confusion the rest of us were suffering from.

"If it's any consolation, even I didn't know my employee could do that," Gally said, emerging from the shadows. "Although I did tell him to get you here as quickly as possible, so I suppose I got what I wanted ultimately."

"Guys, I assume we're getting told which tunnel is which soon," Crystal said, causing me to look around us and spot that there were at least seven tunnel entrances I could see. Indeed, considering it was too dark to see the entire cavern I strongly suspected there were others that I couldn't see with my naked eye. "Cos right now this feels like looking for a needle in a haystack, when you can't even SEE the haystacks."

"That one," Gally said, indicating one to our right that at first seemed pretty unremarkable, until my eyes adjusted and I realised I could just make out a strange silver glow in the air around it. "I've done what I can to negate the spells on this tunnel, but considering the magic an elf alone has at their disposal I would be EXTREMELY careful." He started moving away from us, only to find his way blocked by Petra. "Let me go, I gave you what you wanted."

"How do we know you won't go warn them and ensure

we're walking into an ambush?" Petra asked, placing a firm hand on his shoulder. "Give me a damn good reason why we should trust you."

"I already told you, them staying in charge does me no favours," Gally replied. "Besides, any kind of magic left you fairies can't handle, it's pretty unlikely my skills will be any more help against. I can keep their guards occupied, that way there's less likely to be a response if you guys trigger the alarm."

"Let him go Petra," Selina said, sighing. "I find him as slimy as you do, but...much as I hate to admit it, he has a point." Once Gally had scurried into the darkness, they turned to Marean. "I appreciate your help, but this is our problem to solve, we can't ask you to risk your life here, we have no idea how bad things will be in this castle."

"Okay, but take this," he said, handing Selina a charm on the end of a gold chain. "If things go wrong, just hold this and think my name as clearly as you can, and I will come to you as quickly as my magic will allow me." And then he was gone, teleporting away as if he had never been stood there.

"Come on," Petra said, marching towards the tunnel entrance. "We've wasted plenty of time already, and this place is giving me a bad case of the heebee-jeebies."

We stepped into the tunnel, which although there was no sign of torches or electric lights, was still illuminated by the strange silver glow I had noticed before. For a time, we seemed to be making easy progress, until I realized Crystal had come to a halt a few paces ahead of us.

"Guys...we have a problem," she said, putting her hand

out in front of her. It could only go a short distance before making contact with a silver barrier.

"Same here," Merzel, who had been attempting to backtrack, called from behind me. "Gally lied to us, I knew it."

"You gave that wretch far too much credit," came a voice from ahead of us. The female elf we had faced in Glasswater emerged from the shadows, a terrified-looking Gally held in her vice-like grip. "He was always the... flakiest member of our inner circle, so we suspected he might try to betray us. I thought you should see what your friendship cost the old fool."

"I...I loved you," Gally gasped as the elf drew a short knife from her belt.

"You idiot, that was the mistake you always made, to me you were nothing but a pitiful puppet who outstayed his welcome," the elf said mockingly, slitting Gally's throat with such ease I would've scarcely believed it had happened had she not thrown his dead body aside. She turned back to us. "I'm afraid I can't allow you to interfere in our plans. My...friends will deal with you, I have more important business." As she vanished, I caught sight of something that made my blood run cold: the same eye symbol I had glimpsed when trying to heal the missing teenager.

"She...she has the same magic that attacked the teenagers," I said, feeling myself shaking. "How is that possible? How has the Cartel done all of this without anyone noticing?"

"That's going to have to wait darling," Niana said, her

own voice sounding terrified. "We have *far* bigger problems to worry about."

Before I could ask what she meant, I spotted it myself. It wasn't an ordinary tunnel with magic lighting it, the silver I saw *was* the light. The shadow wasn't cast by the illumination, it was a creature.

Several of them.

Nightstalkers.

Chapter 12

"Crap," Mickey said, the panic in his voice unmistakable. "Clint, one of these things nearly killed you, how the hell are we supposed to fight multiple Nightstalkers?"

"You forget one thing Mickey," I replied, as the energy I could feel surging through my own veins helped me calm my own nerves. "When we faced that Nightstalker, we barely knew magic existed. Now, we know how to wield it," I said, throwing a burst of fire magic at a Nightstalker threatening to sneak up on Petra. To my dismay, though it forced the creature back, the shadowy figure seemed otherwise unaffected by the spell.

"Use your weapons as well as your spells," Selina said, using their sword to deflect a blow aimed at their head. "And remember, don't let their claws touch you, their poison is fatal in all but the rarest circumstances."

"I don't get it," I said as battle was joined, finding myself surrounded by strange combinations of sensations: intense flashes of light threatening to be extinguished by the intense shadows that surrounded the monsters; the loud clang of metal parrying blows, but intense silence answering it. "The Nightstalker we fought before…he was impervious to non-magical blows, we should be struggling."

"You forget one thing Clint," Niana said, driving her sword through the nearest Nightstalker, a look of grim satisfaction on her face as it dissolved into nothing.

"When you fought that creature dark magic was at its strongest, Feth'rael's increased power was making creatures such as these far more dangerous than they would ordinarily be. Whatever else this…Cartel is capable of, even with the power of the Orbs, their power still pales in comparison to that of a death god."

She fired a blast of magic, that looked akin to a ball of lightning, that narrowly missed Crystal but hit the Stalker that was inches away from her square in the chest. Or, at least, as close to a chest as the creatures possessed. "Not that that means we should in any way underestimate them, they still have the advantage in these tunnels."

"Perhaps I can help with that," came Marean's voice from the centre of our group, causing me to turn and find to my surprise that not only had he teleported in, but the Nightstalkers had become frozen where they stood.

"That spell did not freeze time," he said, as if sensing what I and, I suspected, the others thought at that moment. "Merely slowed it enough for those beasts that I can speak to you without you risking being attacked."

He took a deep breath, as if the effort of teleporting to us had drained his strength. "I mean no disrespect to your skills, but if you fight like this the creatures *will* overwhelm you eventually, there are few…if any…spells that can truly destroy them."

"Then what exactly are you proposing?" Selina asked him. "Because I'm pretty damn sure you didn't come here to tell us we were dead, you could've done that before."

"I do not have the time to fully explain," Marean replied. "But Pixies have long had troubles with Nightstalkers, so in order to prevent them threatening the young or the vulnerable one of our number developed a spell which does not destroy them, but banishes them to somewhere a long way from the caster. If I use it, I can clear the worst of the obstacles between you and the Cartel."

"That sounds great," Petra said. "Except I don't need to be able to read your mind to know that it's not that simple a procedure, what's the catch here?"

"There are two problems," the Pixie replied. "I cannot cast the spell instantly, I will need at least five minutes uninterrupted in order to be certain it will work. And during that time, I will need to be protected, when they sense the spell beginning to be cast, I will become their priority target, and I cannot defend myself during that time."

"You need us to distract them?" Petra asked, Marean nodding in response. "I think we can at least manage that. Everyone, form a circle around him, whatever you do, do NOT allow those creatures to break through the ring."

Most of us had become so used to fighting together that the circle had formed almost as soon as the instruction left Petra's lips, Niana as usual ensuring that she was by my side. For a moment I felt a rush of panic as I saw she had put her own blade back in its sheath, until I realised I could already see shimmering green magic forming around her hands, magic that seemed to cause our opponents to shrink away from her.

"How did—"

"How did I do that?" she asked, directing a stream of the magic at a creature that just barely evaded the spell. She couldn't help letting out a chuckle. "I don't know how human society works, but even female fairies not destined for the throne are not expected to stay at home and cook. I was trained in magic, just as my sister was. But where the majority of her training was in protecting the city, mine was in attacking those who threatened it."

She ducked the lunge of a particularly brave Nightstalker, only for the creature to dissolve within an instant of my own sword plunging through what I assumed was its head. Niana stopped for a moment to kiss me on the cheek, an unspoken thank you, before turning her attention back to the fight.

"Of course, when my mother relented and agreed to me learning how to wield these magics, I rather suspect she hoped I'd never have cause to actually *use* any of them."

"I know how you feel," Petra called from the other side of the circle. "There was a time I hoped to become a healer, like my mother, but when...when our parents died, I realised my brother and I had only each other to rely upon, and he was far too young at the time to learn such magic himself. It was when Arkelion stepped in and offered us his aid."

"I hope that spell is nearly ready Marean," Selina said suddenly, her voice sounding as if she was speaking through gritted teeth. "Because this tunnel seems to be getting darker, and I can only imagine that is something to do with our assailants."

"It is almost ready," Marean replied. "If one of you can push them back a short distance, there is one more thing I must do to complete the spell."

Almost as soon as he had finished his request the tunnel filled with a sudden burst of red light, which faded almost as quickly as it had appeared, but we quickly discovered had pushed the creatures around us further down the tunnel in both directions. Looking for an explanation, I found Crystal stood, shaking, red light surrounding her hands.

"We can discuss this later," I said, sensing the others were about to interrogate Crystal about the unusual form her magic took and wanting to spare her the discomfort of having to explain. "Maeran, do you need—" My question was cut off by a burst of light that felt for a moment as if it would blind me, but quickly faded. We all let out a sigh of relief as we realised our assailants had vanished from the tunnel, allowing the odd green glow we had seen glimpses of before to flood our surroundings. I heard a grunt, turning to find Petra helping Marean to his feet. "I take it we have you to thank for what just happened?"

"I…believe humans would call what I just did displacement," Marean replied. "As I could not destroy them, I transported them as far away as I could. It is fortunate that spell was successful, the amount of magical power required to do it is sufficient to prevent me repeating the trick for several hours."

"Marean, you should return to the casino if that weakened you," Petra said.

"No, I am not weak," Marean said, letting go of Petra and standing up unsupported. "Besides," he said, walking over to Gallerya's body and kneeling next to it to close his eyes. "I will not claim that Gally was a perfect creature, not by any stretch of the imagination. But he had a sense of morality, in his own twisted way, that meant he would've protected any who worked for him with his life if he had to. Whatever he did, he didn't deserve to meet his end like this." He stood up again, turning to face us. "I believe this is my fight as much as it is all of yours. Will you accept my aid?"

"He knows this place better than we do," Petra replied. "He's also clearly a pretty skilled magic user, and depending what's waiting for us at the end of the tunnel we might well need all the help we can get."

"Then you're welcome to join us," I said, before blushing slightly when I noticed the look of surprise on the others' faces that I had spoken so quickly. "I'm sorry, I know I'm not the leader here."

Much to my relief there was no dissenting voice to my offer.

"Well, we had best get going," Marean said, beginning to walk ahead of us. "If you had any element of surprise before, I fear my spell will have warned the Cartel we are on our way."

The rest of the journey through the tunnel passed without

incident, causing me to let out a small breath of relief that Gally had at least kept his promise before he had died. Helping my sense of calm was the fact that Niana had silently insisted on taking my hand, I suspected both of us feeling concern at precisely *what* awaited us at the tunnel's end. We did not have to wait long, reaching a set of stone steps at the top of which was an open doorway, leading into a large central entrance hall that appeared unoccupied.

"Wow, this might actually be simple—" Mickey started saying, before he was suddenly cut off.

"Mickey, you know I love you," Selina hissed, loud enough for us all to hear. "But you're about to give the game away to *him*."

I saw where they were pointing, and had to prevent myself letting out a yelp. On the other side of the room, the majority of its facial features obscured by the shadow cast by the nearby stairwell, was a creature that looked vaguely humanoid, but unlike the smaller fairy forms I was used to seeing, this creature's bulk seemed impossibly large, even hunched over.

"An Amarian Troll," Selina cursed under their breath. "They were supposed to have died out centuries ago."

"How does something that big survive so long unnoticed?" I asked.

"Didn't the dragon teach you anything Clint?" Selina asked, raising an eyebrow. "Anything can be hidden, even in plain sight, if you know where and how to avoid detection."

Suddenly I heard a strangled sob from behind me, that I immediately recognised as coming from Crystal, only to quickly spot the cause of her distress. The troll had moved enough to reveal that he was not alone: lying prone, unmistakable by her raven black hair, was Nara. It was impossible to tell from that distance if she was at all injured. I caught a glimpse of something moving and put my hand out, stopping Crystal from proceeding.

"Clint, she...Nara needs our help," Crystal said, sounding hysterical. "Why would you stop me?"

"He did the right thing," Selina replied before I could comment. "Trolls may not be the fastest creatures alive, but if you get too close to it you could be seriously injured, which wouldn't help anyone, but especially not Nara. Luckily for us, I have a plan." She turned to me. "Clint, I want you, Marean and Merzel to keep that thing distracted while I try and figure out if we can get to Nara without having to kill it first."

"Well that doesn't sound dangerous at all," Mickey said. "Are you sure that this is a good idea?"

"Amarians may look slow, but they're more than capable of killing you," Selina replied. "This might be a spectacularly awful idea but...I can't see another option here."

"We'll do it," I said, turning to Marean and Merzel. "Come on, let's see if we can at least get this thing's attention." We passed through the entrance, crossing the room as quietly as we could until we were at what I assumed was a safe distance from the troll. "Hey, troll, we have matters to discuss with you," I said, one hand hovering near the sword at my belt.

The creature's response almost made the colour drain

from my face entirely. As it turned it stood at its full height, half as tall again as the tallest of our number in human form, golden armour placed haphazardly across its body, legs and gauntlets which covered barely half of its immense arms, one of which held a massive warhammer, the other carrying a bladed shield. On its head, showing little more than a pair of intensely red eyes, was a helmet from which jutted a razor-sharp horn.

"Watch out," Marean shouted to me soon enough that I leapt out of the way of its hammer a matter of moments before it shattered flagstones at its impact point. He tried to fire a spell at the troll, but it glanced off the bladed shield as if it was nothing. "Well, I see why they wanted this thing as a bodyguard at least."

"I'm all for a challenge," Merzel said, narrowly escaping a swing aimed straight at his head. "But this is insane, we can't get close enough to inconvenience it, nevermind actually *harm* it. If we've got a plan to take it down it'd be nice if someone could tell me what it is."

"I've got one," Selina said, although it took me a moment to realise they were communicating with us via telepathy. "But…you guys might not like it."

"I'll take any suggestions you can give," I replied telepathically, grimacing as my attempt at a fire spell seemed to dissipate as it hit the troll's armour. "I think this thing can fight far longer than any of us can."

"Mickey and I have…a thing we've been practising during our travels," they replied. "I have a feeling it might be capable of hitting the troll, but to be certain we can put it down…you're going to have to get it to face towards us."

"Selina, you're aware if this fails it'll come straight for you?" Marean's voice asked. "And I'm not convinced any of us three are capable of stopping it if it gets pissed off."

"If that happens, we'll deal with it," Selina replied. "But right now, between that thing's skin and its armour, we're going to die of old age before we so much as scratch it."

"Well, this'll be one to tell the grandkids, assuming we make it out of here," I muttered under my breath, moving directly into the creature's eyeline and using my magic to create a multi-coloured crystal. I let out a sigh of relief when I saw that I had gained its attention, although that lasted only momentarily as I just barely skipped away from the hammer blow, a move which seemed startlingly rapid for such a bulky creature.

"If you want this toy, you'll have to come get it," I said, trying to follow the faint trace of magic the others were letting off and use it to guide me to where I needed to be. As I reached the area directly opposite their hiding place, what followed seemed to occur in slow motion. "*Now* Selina," I shouted, ducking in time to see a bolt of light fly over my head, hitting the troll in a gap in its armour where, I assumed, its heart was. There was an agonising moment as it stood, looking mildly perplexed, before its dead body crashed to the floor, destined never to move again.

"I hate that I had to do that," Selina said, visibly shaken as the others entered the main part of the courtyard. "But the reason Amarian Trolls are so dangerous is that, once they have battle lust, unless you know a very select handful of spells, the only way the battle ends is by you killing it or it killing you."

"Nara," Crystal shouted, drawing our attention away from the corpse to where she was trying to help the Pixie sit up. "Are you…did they…"

"I'm fine," Nara said, wincing slightly as she tried to brush a tear from Crystal's cheek. "Other than roughing me up when they first captured me and a half-assed attempt at an interrogation when I first got here, they pretty much left me alone." She spat a bit of blood on the floor. "I'd sure as hell like to have a few choice words with that elf they call boss though," she said as Crystal helped her unsteadily to her feet.

"No Nara," I said, although I felt ashamed it came out far more harshly than I had intended. "We have no idea what's waiting for us up there, and…no offence, but you're in no state to get in a fight, magical or otherwise."

"Well I'm not leaving her here alone," Crystal said.

"I'm not suggesting you should," I said, offering her a sympathetic smile. "You two go back to Glasswater, we know Akerion is still there, he can help you recover. Please Crystal?"

"Damnit, you're right," she said after a moment. "Just make sure you make the Cartel pay for this."

"Wait," Nara said, just as Crystal was about to cast her spell. "Before you go up there, there's one thing you need to know. There is…something else at work here, something ancient and dangerous. I don't know what it is for certain, just…be careful."

"We'll do our best," I said, giving her shoulder a reassuring squeeze, before they teleported away. I turned towards the central stairs. "Let's just hope whatever's waiting there is less of a pain to stop than the welcoming committee."

We climbed the stairs in silence, the ominous sense of dark magic leading us past darkened corridors and to the top of the stairs, where we were shocked to discover oak doors nearly blown off their hinges. We stepped through, and I felt my stomach lurch at the sight in front of us: at least ten bodies, of fairies, elves, at least one goblin, and a creature I couldn't begin to identify, littered the floor around a ruined table, although there was no visible sign of death until we caught sight of the source of a strange red glow that filled the room. At the far end of the table Car'alean was stood, a terrified looking elvish man trapped in her vicelike grip, although to my horror I could see the life draining from his eyes as I watched.

"Oh good," the elf said, throwing her dead compatriot to the floor and turning to face us. To my astonishment she was no longer armoured, but had instead changed into a long red dress, a purple cloak thrown over her shoulders. "I had feared my…large friend might prevent our reunion, but he at least distracted you long enough to ensure that I could feed at my own leisure."

"*Feed?*" Selina asked, unable to hide her own incredulity at the statement. "What in Gaia's name have you done here? These were your allies."

"Allies?" the elf asked, letting out a sound that was half-laugh, half-cackle. "They were a means to an end, and now they've outlived their purpose."

"So you're feeding on them?" I asked. "If this is how you treat your allies, I would *hate* to see what you do to your enemies. You're like some creepy witch trying to stay young."

"Oh, you misunderstand my point boy," the elf said, the humour vanishing from her face almost instantly. "Although I suppose I could have explained myself better. I'm not siphoning their life and magic for myself, there are far more deserving entities out there. Maybe I can use your beautiful lady friend to give you a...demonstration."

The threat to Niana's safety was enough to make me flip out completely, although my course of action felt like it was being carried out by someone else entirely. I threw a blast of magic at Car'aelean, knocking her off her feet, landing on top of her before she could get up again. Other than a slight bruise on one cheek there was no immediate sign the spell had troubled her in any way, indeed she seemed almost gleeful.

"If I'd known I'd get this response I'd have taunted you sooner," the elf said, smirking at me. "It never ceases to amaze me how easy you humans are to manipulate into doing what we want."

"I've got not time for your games," I said through gritted teeth. "Why would you kill your own cartel? And what the hell is that logo you wear so openly on your cloak?"

"I'm afraid that's not my job to answer," she said, a strange black glow forming around her, which I realised in shock was emanating from the orb that she had used in Glasswater. "I will offer you some advice though." She pulled me close enough that I could feel her breath against my ear. "You were given a warning you chose to ignore. The ravens aren't coming anymore...*they're already here.*"

Before I could question her any further her body dissolved from underneath me, the Orb of Living Death glowing briefly before returning to its normal appearance. I was still in shock as the others came over to me, Niana wrapping her arms around me.

"Considering we won, it sure as hell doesn't feel like it," Mickey said, staring around the room. "What was she doing in here?"

"I don't know," Petra said, walking over and picking up an object that I suddenly realised was the elf's cloak. "But if Clint says he's seen this logo before, I fear the Cartel were but the tip of a particularly nasty iceberg." She passed the cloak onto Selina, whose face seemed to immediately go white as a sheet.

"We need to take this orb back to Akerion," Selina said. "And then we need to figure out whether the Orbs or the Cartel's allies are a bigger threat. Because I have a hunch I've seen this symbol somewhere before and...and if I saw it where I think I did...well, let's just hope I'm wrong."

Chapter 13

We teleported back to Glasswater, Selina carefully transporting the Orb the Elf had once possessed, as soon as we were sure there was nothing we could do to do help at the casino now the Cartel were seemingly all dead. I let out a sigh of relief when we discovered that Nara was awake and looking considerably healthier than she had when Crystal had teleported away with her.

"I ought to thank you all," Nara said, attempting to stand-up, but when she wobbled slightly Crystal gently nudged her back into the chair in which she had been seated. "I have no idea what the Cartel would've done to me if you hadn't come for me."

"We wouldn't leave you at their mercy," I said, offering her my most reassuring smile, even though deep down I didn't feel particularly calm. "Let's face it, Crystal would've never spoken to me again if I'd let you be harmed. Although…unfortunately that's where the good news comes to an abrupt halt. The Cartel are all dead, at least as far as we know anyway."

"You mean you managed to kill them?" Crystal asked,

raising an eyebrow. "Cos if that's true I'm simultaneously both impressed and slightly alarmed."

"We didn't," Selina replied before any of the others could. "That Elf we faced before...she massacred them, she claimed we had no idea what we were *really* facing. And she was wearing this." Selina took the Elf's cloak from me, throwing it on the ground where all of our group could see it. "I have only seen that symbol one place before, but...it is not possible for it to be that group." I realised, watching them out of the corner of my eye, that Selina was visibly shaking.

"What group could scare the bravest person I've ever known?" Mickey asked, resting a comforting hand on her shoulder.

"The Cult of the Drakoni," Arkelion said, the elderly fairy suddenly appearing in our midst, mere feet from the cloak. "That symbol was...you humans would describe it as their calling card. I may not have been alive during their era, but every fairy book on the dangers of dark magic has that symbol in it somewhere."

"But that's impossible," Selina said, unable to hide the incredulity in their tone of voice. "That group were wiped out centuries ago, how the hell would *any* symbol of theirs find its way to 21st Century America?"

"It is not so unlikely," Prince Akerian said, moving into the circle, a grim look unmistakable on his face. "This city... Glasswater...is proof by itself of the temptation of dark magic, all it would need was one person too wicked or naive to recognise the threat of the former bearers of that symbol and this would spread easily enough. Plus, if this...*Cartel* were so desperate to gain control of the Orbs, it is possible they saw themselves as some form of successor to the original cult."

"This all feels too easy though," Selina said through gritted teeth. "Surely they would be aware there were fairies who knew the meaning of that symbol, even now?"

"Selina," Mickey said, slipping his hand into hers. "We'll figure this out. Well, more like you will, being the smartest person in this room by a country mile," he said, the last comment making Selina bury their face in his shirt, I suspected in an attempt to hide how red their face had turned. "This does highlight one thing though," Mickey continued. "Between the messages from the Ravenspire, the missing kids and now this… mess in Las Vegas, we have to locate the other Orbs as a matter of urgency surely?"

"That's a great idea on paper," Niana replied. "But we don't have the first idea where to look for them, and I don't know about the rest of you, but I don't want to risk them being unleashed again, not when we haven't the first idea what any of these things is capable of doing."

"There is a way," Marek, who had been stood to one side with his arms wrapped around him, suddenly said. "Or, at least, a potential option. Have you all forgotten one of the reasons we came here? The Timeless Oak, if we could locate it—"

"That's an old wives' tale told to comfort scared children," Petra scoffed. "And even if the stories as to what it was capable of hold even a fragment of truth to it, you are looking for *one tree* in the middle of the largest park in New

York, one that would likely have wards and Gaia only know what else to prevent just anyone from gaining access to it."

"I can tell you where the tree is," Arkon said. "Unfortunately…the few of this city who could warn you what awaits you there are long dead. I cannot come with you however, this city…with the Orb gone I must do what I can to restore this city to a liveable condition. Maybe, one day, life will even return to this place."

"You don't need to explain," Selina said, walking over to the prince and placing a hand gently on his shoulder. "If we could, we would stay to aid you in your work."

"Take this," Akerian said, placing something in Selina's hand. "If, at any point, you require my aid this charm will warn me. I promise I will come if you ask, you have earnt my loyalty with your actions here." He turned to the rest of us, a faint smile on his face. "The Timeless Oak is one of the most sacred places for fairies in this part of the world, there are fae old enough to be your grandparents who have never had a chance to gaze within it." He raised a hand, a glowing aura forming around it as an image formed on the floor. At first it appeared to be little more than a standard map of Central Park, until I noticed that strange glowing lines were forming within the park. "Most of the fairies who once occupied the Park may have long since departed, but their magic is there if you know where to look. For you, your destination is…there." The lines seemed to briefly shine brighter, the pulse directed at something that might not have stood out otherwise: next to a war memorial stood a lone tree, one whose name seemed unusually blurred. "There is a magical order sworn to protect the tree, they believed that by not attempting to hide it humans would see no reason to investigate further."

"It's like I said when you wondered why the Glade had never been located," Niana said to me. "The right magic can make something hidden to humans if they do not wish to see it."

"Then that is our destination," Petra said, stepping closer so she could get a clear look at the map. "Master Arkelion, do you want to come with us?"

"No," the older fairy said, shaking his head. "This is well within you young ones' ability to deal with, besides I can see what I can do to locate the orbs myself." He walked over to where Selina had dropped the cloak, picking it up gingerly. For the briefest moment I thought I saw a burst of strange purple light around him, but it was gone so quickly I assumed the poor lighting of the cavern had tricked my eyes. "I will also look into this symbol, see if I can find an explanation for how it fell into the possession of an elf and her cronies. Good luck, all of you," he said, in the next instant vanishing in front of our eyes.

"Are you okay?" Niana asked, causing me to realise I had zoned out briefly, the others already gathered around Petra, although the Prince and Arkelion had both vanished.

"Yeah...I'm fine," I replied, although I felt about as convinced by my response as Niana looked, but she gave my hand a reassuring squeeze. "Come on, we've got a magical tree to visit."

When we appeared in Central Park there was a collective

sigh of relief that the few locals nearby didn't seem to have noticed our sudden appearance. Sixty metres to our left we could immediately saw what we were looking for: the memorial was topped by a solitary soldier, a handful of wreaths and a pair of bouquets dotted around its base. But, as tall as the memorial was, what lay beyond it was far more impressive. While the trunk was nothing particularly remarkable, its branches seemed to reach into the sky far above the ground.

"I don't sense any magic around here," Petra said, her hand lingering near her sword. "But we ought to be careful, something about this place feels…odd."

We started walking towards the tree, not far from the rope that surrounded the memorial, I felt a slight feeling of static electricity pass across my skin, giving me a mild fright, swiftly followed by a feeling of shock at the change that had occurred around us. The memorial had disappeared, and the leaves of the tree were suddenly silver coloured, its trunk now containing a doorway only just discernible among the grain of the bark.

"I…I don't understand," I said, struggling to get my thoughts in some form of order. "This isn't the same place we just were, otherwise humans would be stumbling upon this randomly almost every day."

"You children have barely begun to understand what magic is capable of," came a voice from behind us. We spun around as one, finding ourselves confronted by a tall slender figure. It had a featureless white mask covering its face, behind which a pair of piercing green eyes could just be glimpsed, along with dark blue hair. It was dressed in a long black robe, beneath which could be glimpsed heavily tattooed arms, tattoos that formed sentences in a language I could make no sense of. "What you have entered is an effect of a spell called Timelock. In a sense we are still within your world, but we are...out of sync with it. The spell has been designed to prevent access to those without fae blood in their veins." The figure continued walking through our group, eventually stopping to turn to face us. "The Order of Illithas does not allow just anyone access to the Great Oak, state your purpose and I will judge whether you are worthy."

"The Orbs of the Drakoni are loose in the world again," Petra said, stepping forward. "If the stories of the power that rests here are correct, it may be our only hope of locating the relics before they fall into the wrong hands." The figure showed so little response I felt my concern rising. Petra took a step closer to our mystery interrogator. "My parents told me legends of the great guardian Illithas and his hero's death against the Drakonite Cult, you must be aware of the threat those spells pose, we would not ask this of you if we felt there was another option."

"I believe you," the figure said, moving aside and waving his hand in the direction of the door, which opened to reveal a black void beyond. "The Stone of Illithas will answer your question, but be warned, the tree can show you all the potential futures, it is...better for your own mental health that you avoid anything other than the stone. Once your work here is done, I will aid you in returning to your own world."

"You may as well go," I said to Petra. "I can't imagine

there's much space there, and you know the information we need better than anyone else."

"No pressure then," Petra said, letting out a nervous laugh. "I guess I'll see you shortly." She set off towards the tree, the door seeming to disappear in front of her, only causing her a momentary pause before she stepped inside. "Guys, there's plenty of space in here," she called out. "I think you'd better come see this."

Mickey and I shared a confused glance, before we all walked up to the opening in the trunk, stepping through to a collective gasp at what faced us: although the interior was mostly in darkness there was a definite sense our surroundings stretched far above us. The only visible detail in the room was suspended in a beam of light with no obvious source, a circular rock, on which could just be glimpsed intricate writing in a language I couldn't begin to identify, nevermind make sense from.

"Remember what he said outside," Petra said, evidently guessing the confusion we all felt at the scene. "Compared to his order we are still novices when it comes to the uses of the magical arts." She took a step towards the rock, extending a hand towards it. The object seemed to pulse with golden light in response. "If your magic is as powerful as I've been told it is, your order is aware of what the Drakonite weapons are capable of. You are the only way we have of finding them before they fall into the wrong hands. Please, do something." For a few moments there was no response, but just as I felt myself losing hope there was a sudden burst of light, the stone replaced by a giant map of the world, upon which bursts of golden light were slowly revealing themselves.

"Guys, I don't want to panic you," Selina said, "but that map has two Orbs in Europe and one in Africa. If that's true, then why did the kidnappers only target American kids?"

"You're assuming the attackers *knew* there were Orbs outside America," Petra replied. "Hell, we don't even know if all these kidnappings were carried out by the same people." She was silent for a few moments, before sighing. "I don't suppose any of you have some paper and a pencil? There's not a chance in hell I'm remembering all of this off the top of my head."

"Here you go," Marek said, taking a sketchbook and pencil out of his bag, before blushing as he realised we were all looking at him. "What? I like drawing, these things come in handy."

"Marek, never apologise for indulging your creativity," Petra said. "Now, give me a bit of quiet, I need to focus."

As she set to work, I could tell the others felt restless, I felt it too. There was nowhere obvious to sit, so at that moment we appeared more reminiscent of a particularly unenthusiastic indoor rave. I was just beginning to zone out when I heard it.

"*We wish...to show you...*"

It wasn't one of the others, I was certain of it, but at first, I couldn't tell from which direction the voice was coming from, until it appeared again.

"*Beyond the stone...the Star Mirror awaits you...*"

It was as if I was in a trance, my legs leading me away

from the group and into the shadows, although I hadn't got far before I saw it. Seemingly floating in mid-air, its surface seeming to be unnaturally lit in the otherwise darkened room, stood an ornately framed mirror. Almost directly in front of my eyeline was a pulse of green light, which I found my hand drawn towards…

…In the next moment I was no longer in the Oak, instead stood in a strange room, a man chained to the wall, a figure with its back to me, wearing a long-hooded cloak, deep in conversation with him, although I caught only one part, which seemed to echo as if I was stood in an impossibly large chamber.

"No…no, it's impossible, you can't be here, I saw you die."

Even as my mind tried to adjust to what was happening my surroundings changed again. Now I was stood in the centre of a ruined building, a matter of feet from two bloodied figures. One was a young man, a strange mechanical arm just visible over his shoulder. Although the other appeared at first glance to be human, its skin was aquamarine, a breathing apparatus visible on the suit it wore. The human was holding onto the other's motionless form tightly.

"Sark, I'm sorry I waited this long but…I need you to know, I…I love you, please…you have to stay with me."

I felt my emotions welling up, even as my surroundings changed again. What on Earth was going on? This time I was stood in a plain looking house, the only other occupant a stockily built woman with dark skin, who at that moment was finishing writing something on a piece of paper. She was just placing it in the pocket of her jacket when there was a knock at the door. Grabbing a gun from a nearby desk she approached the door and opened it, but for some reason I couldn't see the person stood outside, even as the woman spoke with an accent I just about recognised as being South African.

"Oh, it's just you, you could frighten a girl turning up like this. I've got something to show you, it's…wait, what are you—"

Before I could hear the rest, my surroundings changed, but this change shocked me most of all. I was no longer on Earth but floating above a planet which even a cursory glance told me wasn't Earth, but if that had surprised me what I saw as I turned around made the hair on the back of my neck stand up. It appeared to be a giant octopus, but instead of eyes or anything recognisably biological the structure was metallic, and I could have sworn I could sense waves of energy pouring outwards from it.

"It's beautiful, isn't it?" came a voice out of nowhere, seeming to echo around me. *"I only wish I could claim responsibility for its existence."*

It took me a moment to realise the voice was addressing me, not that the realization made me feel any calmer.

"Illithas?" I called out. "Why pick me to show these to?"

"I'm afraid I'm not Illithas," the voice replied. *"Although you are correct that I brought you here. We have watched you with…curiosity."*

"We?" I asked. "And who the hell is *we* when they get out of bed in the morning? And why show me these, unless you want me to prevent these events from occurring?"

"You cannot change these events boy," the voice snarled.

"What you have seen is the future, just not your future. There is so much more to reality that you have yet to comprehend Clint, although I expect that to change soon."

It felt in that moment as if the very blood in my veins had filled with ice. "How...how do you know my name? What the hell are you?"

"I'm afraid I cannot tell you what we are, not yet," the voice replied. *"As I said we have watched your developments closely, as we have all those whose actions...interest us. I promise you you will have your eyes opened soon enough, although..."* Suddenly a patch of shadow appeared in front of me, the intense red eyes that stared at me identical to those I had seen when trying to heal the missing girl, *"...in a sense, we are already familiar with each other. If you want the answer to the horrors you currently face, you must find the Spire. I just hope you are ready for what you are going to discover."*

The last thing I knew I felt an intense headache, unable to prevent myself from losing consciousness...

"Clint, can you hear me?"

For a moment I panicked, until I realised the voice I heard was Niana's. I opened my eyes, finding her concerned face looking down at me.

"Clint, you're awake," she said, hugging me close. "What happened? You disappeared, we heard a crash and you...we took you out of the tree, I feared its magic had affected you in some way."

"Niana, I..." I paused, trying to make sense of the jumble of memories in my head. "I'm not sure if I told you what happened in there that you'd believe a word I say. It's...we need to talk to the others, there have been developments." I sat up, seeing all but Mickey were stood nearby watching me. "I'm sorry, I've disturbed our pla—"

"Guys, you need to see this," Mickey called from within the tree. "We have a...development, and it's a pretty bad one."

Niana and I shared a concerned look, before she helped me to my feet, leading the rest back inside the tree. Mickey was stood in front of the map, which appeared almost identical...but one of the markers was no longer gold, but flashing a dark red colour. "That's...that's Mount Rushmore," I stammered out, at that moment wishing my memory of US geography wasn't so good. "But what does that mean?"

"There is an Orb powering up there," Selina replied, the panic in her voice unmistakable. "We need to go, *now*, and hope to whatever higher power we believe in that we're not already too late."

Chapter 14

We didn't waste a moment in heading for Mount Rushmore. Nara joined us despite my own concerns after she pointed out she was the only one of us capable of sensing dark magic before it was too late. I wasn't sure what to expect when we arrived, but I felt my heart sink when we were confronted with an area milling with tourists and the occasional tour guide, only mildly tempered by there being no clear sign of dark magic anywhere.

"Guys," Mickey said, breaking the silence. "This has got disaster written all over it, if the Orb from Glasswater went off here—"

"Mickey darling, that's not how the Orbs work," Selina said, interrupting him but offering their most reassuring smile. Or attempting to anyway. "No two Orbs contain the same spell, we could be dealing with absolutely anything. We do need to get everyone we can away from here though, so I'm open to suggestions."

"We need to be careful how we do this," I said. "If we cause a mass panic, even unintentionally, we could make this situation far *far* worse. Selina, do you think you could persuade the guards to evacuate the area without too many problems?"

"I...I'm surprised I'm saying this, but I think I do," Selina replied, barely managing to hide a grin. "But I'm going to need some help. Mickey, Crystal, you're with me. I suggest everyone else spreads out, in case we can get any idea where this thing is, even if we can't be sure what it's going to do."

Before I, or any of the others, could question the plan Selina and the other two had vanished. For a few moments we were stood looking at each other, none of us seemingly sure as to what the next move should be.

"We need a signal," Petra finally said, breaking the silence. "We're best off splitting up for this search, but if we find something it'd be good to have a way of tipping each other off if we're lucky and locate this before anything bad happens."

"Chocolate flavoured meatballs," Marek blurted out, before looking thoroughly embarrassed, his cheeks flushing bright red. "Well, that sounded funny in my head."

"Maybe we should just stick to communicating telepathically," I said, trying and just barely succeeding in keeping a straight face. "Otherwise we may as well be shouting 'Fire!' in a packed cinema, with about as bad an end result. Make sure Nara is the person you keep in contact with though, she's as close to a dark magic alarm as we can get, let's just hope it doesn't come to that."

We spread out, those of the group I could see trying to avoid either drawing attention from the tourists or covering the same areas of ground by mistake. My initial optimism didn't last long however, and I was on the verge of declaring it a lost cause when I noticed a strange dark brown root lying on the ground, one which seemed to be growing in front of my eyes. It was when I stepped towards it though that I heard the scream, looking up to see a young man I didn't recognise trapped in the branches of a tree that was slowly growing around him.

"*I saw*," Nara sent telepathically before I could attempt to contact her. "*Everyone, converge on it, even if it's not the Orb something about this feels…off.*"

I needed no further encouragement, but even as I reached the scene, I could feel the dark magic rolling off the tree in waves, to the point that I felt a wave of nausea that only seemed to ease when I took a step back. Even so, I could *see* the darkness radiating outwards, something I had never experienced before.

"What the hell kind of dark magic is *this*?" Marek asked. "If it wasn't for the light show I'd think this was just a plant someone had fed too much." Fire started to form around his hands, only for Petra to place a hand on his arm. "What are you doing? I was going to free him."

"That won't help," Petra said. "For once this is dark magic I know…or at least I know magic very similar to it."

"It's called The Hunger," Selina said, kneeling down next to one of the roots, flinching as they reached towards it. "Petra is right, if you try and launch anything like fire at it, that'll just make it stronger. The more you feed it, the stronger it becomes. And yet this…this is somehow worse."

"What do you mean?" I asked, realising they had given up any pretence of hiding the fear in their voice.

"The Hunger is mostly mentioned in relation to granting a form of immortality," Selina replied. "It keeps the wielder alive by drawing the energy into their body, so ordinarily you could fix it by at least knocking out the person producing the spell. But this…the spell isn't linked to this guy, it's possible the Orb itself is powering the spell, which will make dispelling it even more—"

"Selina," Mickey said softly, placing a hand on their shoulder. "You're not alone here, we'll find a way."

"Help…me…"

We all spun around in surprise, realising the voice belonged to the man trapped in the expanding tree, a man who seemed to be weakening before our eyes.

"We'll…we'll help you," Selina said, trying to calm themselves down as much as the poor man. "I'm going to find a way of releasing you from that."

"You…can't," the man said, gasping for breath. "I can hear it…in my head, it's feeding off the life around here, if you can't stop it now, it will feed on everyone here, making it stronger. You…you have to kill me, it won't stop it, but…it'll slow the expansion down."

"There has to be another way," I said, looking between Selina and the prisoner. "He's innocent in all this, he doesn't deserve to die. Nara, Selina, there must be something you can do."

"Unfortunately there isn't," Nara replied. "And I finally realised why he'd know how this spell works. He…he's one of the missing teenagers." I stepped closer, and suddenly realised Nara was right. There was a distinctive jagged birthmark on his right cheek, one that I realized had stood out among the files we examined. Although he looked far weaker than he had in the photo. "If we can end his suffering, wouldn't it be more immoral *not* to do so?" Nara asked.

I felt my heart sink as I considered what Nara said. I wanted, desperately, to voice an alternative that would avoid more death, but I couldn't. She was right.

"I'll do it," Petra said suddenly. "I know a...relatively painless spell that can do it, but I don't advise you watch what happens. Keep an eye on the surrounding area, there's a chance we'll be able to see where the Orb is once he dies. That...or things will go downhill pretty damn quickly."

Most of us spread out, although I noticed Niana stayed close to me, not that I was about to complain. We were on the edge of a hill, looking down upon the area in front of Rushmore, which was emptier than it had been when we first arrived, but there was still a considerable crowd of tourists. Although I expected a sound to signify Petra's work was done, it was the scene in front of us which gave the game away. More dark purple roots spread outwards from a large tree I could've sworn wasn't there before. But that wasn't the most worrying sign: Hovering above the branches of the tree, solidifying as we watched, was a ball of energy the same colour as the roots.

"*You shouldn't meddle in something that isn't your business children,*" said a voice which sounded both in my mind but also coming from somewhere alarmingly close by.

"What...what the hell was that?" Niana asked, clutching the side of her head, something I had the urge to do myself as I felt an intense pain in my skull. "I've never felt telepathy like that before."

"I'm not sure you're going to like the answer," Petra replied, I turned to notice she had turned white as a sheet. She pointed in the direction we had been looking moments ago. "I've heard myths about this, but I thought they were the ravings of fantasists. That spell doesn't have a caster, I don't know how but…it has gained some form of sentience. We need to evacuate this place *now*, I have no idea what magic like this is capable of. *Nobody* does."

"Merzel, Mickey, Marek, find the nearest authority figure and tell them what's going on," Selina said. "Well…maybe not the whole story, but at least enough for them to get the civilians as far away from here as possible. The rest of us…I guess we're about to make a bit of history, let's just hope we live long enough to feel impressed by it."

The difference in air around the growths was almost suffocating as I materialised in the middle of it all, barely able to see in the distance the organised chaos of the attempted evacuation. I had to take a few moments to compose myself, a wave of nausea pouring over me.

"Clint, I'm here," Niana said, sounding distant until I felt her hand take mine in a firm grip. "Geez, fighting a literal God was less of a problem than this was," she said, her laugh dying as quickly as it started. "Come on, we need to get closer, just…let's avoid stepping on those roots."

Niana's suggestion was easier said than done, not only did it seem that the roots were growing every time we looked at them, but they seemed to have sensed us, and thus were moving towards us. We dodged though them, both of us attempting to swipe with our swords at the appendages but to no effect. It seemed the air was threatening to overwhelm us, but just as I felt on the urge of collapse, we reached where the entity was, where the air seemed to be clearer, the rest of the group having reached it too. At the centre of our group was...describing it was difficult. There was a hint of a humanoid shape, but it seemed to be formed of some form of shadow.

"Let me guess, you're here to kill me?" the entity asked. "If you think you can kill magic, you're more foolish than the Drakoni, even at their most arrogant."

"Wait, you've been alive since the Drakoni?" I asked, feeling my hand drift towards my sword. "I mean...I'm no expert, but surely no spell could last *that* long?"

"What, you think the Drakoni created these spells out of thin air?" the entity asked, laughing deeply. "Some of them they did, but mine...They thought I was a parasite, but my...'hosts' eventually become my slaves. Now though...now I am free to take whatever life I wish."

"We can't allow you to do that," Petra said, her voice shaking slightly. "This ends right here, *right now*."

"I've already told you, you cannot kill magic," the creature said, its gaze sweeping across our group. "What could you imagine you are capable of doing which would stop me?"

I expected a sarcastic response, but all I saw initially was a nod pass between Petra and Selina, before the former turned back to the entity.

"If the Drakonite Cult was as weak as you claim, why would you aid them?"

"It was convenient," the creature replied. "Our minions, the Nightstalkers, can find us a certain amount of food, but it's easier to find our meals…directly." I felt a shiver down my spine at the mention of the Nightstalkers, the memory of the one that had nearly killed me, never mind the attack in the desert tunnels, still fresh in my mind. "I ought to thank that fool for freeing me, centuries trapped in a confined space can get boring very quickly. Would you really force a living creature to live like that again?"

"I'm guessing we can't just politely ask you to go back where you came from?" Marek asked, just barely managing to utter a half-hearted laugh.

"I'm permanently linked to that Orb," the creature responded. "So no, the days where you could simply banish me back to my 'home' are long since gone."

"Well, I guess we'll just have to do the next best thing," Selina growled, suddenly appearing behind our enemy, a Drakonite Orb in one hand. "I *really* hope this works, otherwise this is gonna go downhill really quickly."

What happened next was simultaneously extraordinary and frightening. The creature turned towards Selina, a burst of dark magic forming around its fingertips, but as it curled its 'arm' towards them the magic began to siphon towards the Orb, the entity letting out a terrifying, unearthly scream which seemed to reverberate all around us.

"Fools, this isn't over," its voice called out. "You think you know darkness…he will show you what darkness truly is. And then…then *they* will feed on the scraps. I will enjoy…" His rant finally ended as the last of the entity flowed into the Orb, everyone letting out a sigh of relief that the strange tentacles vanished at the same moment.

"At least that…Ahh," Selina stopped mid-sentence, falling to their knees as a strange purple cord seemed to spread up her hand. "Something…something is very wrong."

"We'll get you help," Mickey said, wrapping his arms around Selina. "Whatever this is, we'll fix it."

"Mickey, you don't understand," Selina said, shaking uncontrollably as they leant against Mickey. "Touching the Orb…I can see the other relics, there is a small amount of good news, but an awful lot of bad news too. I couldn't sense six of the relics, like someone or something had turned them off…or at the very least stored them somewhere the Orb couldn't detect them. But the remaining three…they're getting stronger; I don't know for certain what is coming, but I fear it is big…and dangerous…and…" With no warning Selina's eyes suddenly fluttered shut, Mickey catching them before they could fall to the floor.

"Selina?" Mickey asked, as I noticed the purple strands seemed to have covered her lower arm entirely. "Please, someone help her, she's alive, but—"

"We can take it to Akerion," Petra said. "He knows these Orbs better than anyone, he can help her."

"No," Nara said forcefully. "I'm sorry Petra, but I'd be more comfortable taking her to my mother. She is the best healer I've ever met, we can take the Orb to Akerion when we are sure Selina is safe." I felt myself let out a breath of relief that Petra made no attempt to argue. But as we prepared to form a teleport circle Nara grabbed my arm, turning me to face her. "Clint, once we have reached my home you and I need to have a conversation."

"How come?" I asked, shocked by the fact she wasn't even trying to hide the alarm in her voice.

"I can't say here," she replied. "But I think we both know something about this isn't right, and I fear we're running out of time to figure out how to stop it."

Chapter 15

In the circumstances I was glad we teleported to Nara's home city in a matter of moments, although we materialised outside an entrance I didn't recognise, set into a white marble wall, on top of which was stood a lanky older fairy, one hand resting on his sword. He seemed momentarily worried at our appearance, till his eyes alighted upon Nara, stood at the front of our group.

"Lady Nara, I didn't notice you there," the guard said, regaining some degree of composure. "I'm not used to you using the Bayan gate to the city, otherwise I—"

"Captain Irios, ordinarily I'd appreciate your passion for tradition, but we have an emergency." As she finished, she moved aside, Petra taking a step forward. In her arms at that moment was Selina's unconscious form, the tentacles still spreading up her arm. "We require my mother's aid, it is a matter of urgency."

"Of course, m'lady," Irios replied, signalling with his hand to someone behind the wall, the gate opening to reveal a narrow corridor between buildings, before Irios vanished further into the city.

"I didn't know you were a Lady," Merzel said to Nara, trying to stifle a laugh. "Do you want us to bow to you now?"

"I don't have a title of any description as long as my mother remains on the throne," Nara replied irritably. "I'm pretty sure I've pointed this out to Irios at least once a year since I turned ten, but he insists. Right now though, Selina is our priority, I'll take you to the Rooms of Healing."

The route we took felt a little eerie. Although we could hear the sound of children somewhere in the near distance, the passageways we took were almost entirely unoccupied, beyond the occasional guard passing us. Even once we entered the small tower that was evidently our destination the only possible sign of other life was that the doors to some rooms were shut. We finally stopped at a room that, as we stepped inside, I realized was the same one I had woken up in following the battle with Feth'rael. As Nara helped Petra to lay Selina on the bed there was a clicking sound approaching the door, and I turned to discover a female fairy who, despite being shorter and displaying the first signs of ageing, was almost identical to Nara. Queen Asira's warm smile vanished as soon as she caught a glimpse of the bed, turning to another female fairy stood in the doorway and uttering something I couldn't understand, before turning back to us.

"I had thought...or at the very least *hoped*...I would never see this magic again," Asira said, walking to the bed as the rest of us stepped aside, a golden glow forming around her hands as she took hold of Selina's arm.

"You've seen this before?" Nara asked, catching me off-guard as I realised she seemed surprised at the revelation.

"Not this exact spell, although I have heard of it," Asira replied, the glow spreading all the way up the infected arm. "Unfortunately there are other dark magic spells that can have a similar effect." She looked around, offering a reassuring smile when she saw our panic. "You brought her here rapidly, she is in safe hands with me, I promise."

"Mother, are the Pools of Reflection available?" Nara asked. "I need to speak to my friends in private, plus it'd be best if we're not distracting you while you're using your magic like this."

"As far as I know, yes," Asira replied. "Don't worry, I will send someone to find you once Selina's condition is more stable."

This time, rather than heading into the city, Nara led us through a trapdoor and into an underground passage which came to an end at a large cavern. For a moment the amount of illumination in the room confused me, seeming impossible for an underground cavern, until I realised the room was dominated by two large pools which seemed to glow with an ethereal light.

"The water is enchanted," Nara said, walking over and sitting down with her feet in the water, the rest of us quickly joining her. The sensation was remarkable, first causing an intense tingling feeling, before it felt as if a pleasantly warm liquid was washing through my body. "It's a good thing the spell on these lakes has never been dispelled, my mother has freely admitted the knowledge of what it actually is has long since been lost to history."

For several minutes we all sat in silence, my own eyes drawn to the unusual patterns playing across the ceiling directly over my head. It almost felt as if we could have sat there for hours, but then Mickey let out a deep sigh.

"So, why did you bring us here exactly?" he asked. "Not that I don't appreciate the surroundings, but I don't think you brought us here for a bit of rest and relaxation."

"You're right," Nara said, sighing too as she ran a hand through her short red hair. "There's been something I've been worrying about for a while, but…I get the impression Clint has similar concerns, so I realised we need to *all* consider this: I strongly suspect this situation is being manipulated, hell, that it's been manipulated since before we even became involved in this hunt."

"And you're basing this on what exactly?" Marek asked, watching her intently.

"The way the weapons activated," Nara replied. "The Orb under Glasswater came online due to dark magic in its proximity, and we have no reason to think The Hunger couldn't become active of its own volition if it's tapping into sentient entities. But the rest…Even if we accept that Madeline is the rare human with magical ability, there's no way all the kids on the list have magical talents. And even if they did, these Orbs aren't designed to be activated by just any magic user. Which means—"

"That someone set this all up," I said, closing my eyes and grimacing.

"Someone with more dark magical ability than I've *ever* come across," Petra said, resting her head in her hands. "There's no way this is good news. But what can we even do? We don't know where to even start looking for anyone doing this."

"Our first priority has to be tracking down the remaining Orbs," Mickey said with enough force that we all turned to look at him, the anger unmistakable in the fierce look he gave each of us. "Whoever did this seriously hurt Selina, but if we don't secure those weapons there will be many more dead. Once we're sure they're safe, *then* we can go after our enemy."

"That was my thought too," Nara said. "Let's just hope there are no more dark sec—" She sprang up as we all heard a set of footsteps approaching, but it was only a young male fairy, dressed in armour he only just seemed tall enough to wear, who was shifting nervously from foot to foot. "Is my mother summoning us?" The young fairy didn't speak, only offering a quick nod in reply. "Come on," Nara said, turning back to us. "Hopefully Selina is better."

When we got back to the room, I felt relieved to see Selina sat up in bed, a piece of paper stretched out across their lap, Asira stood by the room's only window. Mickey rushed over to the bed and wrapped Selina in a hug, Selina kissing his forehead before offering us all a warm smile.

"Well, at least I have a tattoo finally," they said, lifting their arm enough to reveal that although the Orb had been removed there were still marks running from their wrist to their elbow. "I promise it looks worse than it is."

"Where's the Orb?" Petra asked. "There is somewhere

we can take it that will keep it safe, I should do that before we forget."

"There," Asira replied, pointing to a desk in the corner of the room on top of which was sat an object covered in a colourful cloth. "I do not wish to have evil like that in my city for any longer than necessary."

"I will take it," Petra said, walking over and picking it up. "Don't worry, if you locate another orb, I'll rendezvous with you easily enough." With that Petra vanished in the blink of an eye.

"What were you drawing?" Marek asked Selina, bringing my attention back to the bed, where I noticed they'd resumed sketching on it.

"Well, this was likely an accidental side-effect of the whole being comatose thing," Selina replied, chuckling. "But while me and that...thing were linked, I got another glimpse of where the remaining three Orbs are located. I hate to break this to you, but it is *not* all good news on that front."

"How about we start with the good news?" Asira asked. "I feel like you could all do with some positivity currently."

"One of the Orbs is in the Sahara Desert," Selina said, waiting till we'd walked over to the bed to show us a trio of maps she'd drawn. "I don't know how the hell it got there, but it seems to be in the vicinity of a deserted fairy colony called Al-Bahein."

"The Sahara is the *good* news?" Merzel asked incredulously. "How bad is the bad option that the middle of the desert is a *positive*?"

"Well, the next one is on the Great Wall of China,"

Selina replied. "Well, more accurately in the vicinity of the Wall. That could be…interesting, the fairies in that region aren't renowned for welcoming outsiders. But the third could be the biggest headache of all, because I'm not absolutely certain where it even is."

"I don't understand," Mickey said, squeezing Selina's hand. "If you got such precise locations for the other two, how come that one in particular caused you such problems?"

"I can't be certain," Selina replied. "I don't know whether someone is moving it, or whether some form of spell has been cast to hide it from magical tracking, but I can't trace it to anywhere more specific than somewhere around the Italian Mediterranean coast, possibly to the north."

"And that is where the problem comes in," Asira said, sighing as she looked between us. "Are you so ignorant of the history of the fae? The location Selina is describing is insignificant to modern history, but it is in close proximity to Mirallein Island. Are any of you aware what that means, or must I turn this into a history lesson?"

"Oh no…" Nara said, sinking into a nearby chair, shaking slightly as Crystal put an arm around her shoulders.

"What is it?" I asked, looking between Nara and the Queen, before I felt Niana squeeze my hand.

"Darling," Niana said. "Remember when we mentioned the Drakoni made a last stand where they were wiped out? Mirallein was the location of said battle." I suddenly realised I could feel her shaking, so I squeezed her hand in an attempt to help her regain composure. "There's no way that's a coincidence, is there?"

"We can't worry about that right now," Selina replied. "Especially if we can't be sure where the Orb is. Much as I can't quite believe I'm saying this, the Sahara is the best option for you guys to go to first, at least because it's the one with the least likelihood you'll run into potentially... unfriendly locals."

"You say that like you're not coming with us," I said, although I could see they still looked unsteady.

"We don't know what's waiting in the desert," Selina said. "The last thing you need is to be worrying about me. Besides, I need to check a few things with Spider and, no offence, but I feel like the internet in the middle of the Sahara is...not great." They squeezed Mickey's hand. "You should go with them, I'll be fine and I know you'll be bored if you're stuck here watching me working on my laptop. Besides, hopefully I'll feel better by the time we're heading for China."

"I'll tell you all about it when we get back," Mickey replied, pulling Selina into a kiss heated enough it only stopped when Crystal let out an embarrassed cough. "Sorry, I guess I got a little...carried away there," Mickey said, rubbing the back of his neck.

"Let's get going," Niana said, grabbing my hand. "God only knows what the two lovebirds will get up to if we wait any longer."

The wave of heat which hit us as we appeared in the Sahara was so strong that, even in relatively light clothing, I almost instantly felt overdressed, only slightly relieved by the realisation I wasn't alone in suffering judging by the faces the others were pulling. At first there seemed to be nothing other than sand and undulating dunes around us, but then I noticed a familiar magical glint, and as we approached it, I realised I could glimpse half-covered ruins poking out of the sand.

"Nara, are you sensing anything?" I asked as we tried to find any way to look at the ruins closer. "There's not even a shrinking spell here, I can't imagine there's been any form of life around here for a very long time."

"There's not even a trace of dark magic here," she replied, the frustration audible in the tone of her voice. "I don't know whether that's better or *worse* than if it was obvious. Be on your guard, I'd rather this spell didn't reveal itself by killing one of us."

"Um...I don't suppose that would count as dark magic?" Marek called out.

We all turned to where he was stood a short distance from the group, at first unable to see anything out of the ordinary. Lurching towards us, like something out of a horror movie, were what at first glance might appear normal humans and fairies, but some were in varying states of decay and I felt certain at least one was nothing more than a skeleton.

"Oh great, necromantic spells," Nara said, as we looked around and realised more were closing in, surrounding us. "So...I think it's safe to say we have a problem right now."

Chapter 16

The sound of all of us drawing our blades seemed to reverberate around the dunes. Petra loosed off a fireball at one of the zombies which made it disintegrate, but even as we were celebrating another zombie appeared at the top of the sand dunes.

"I can't believe I need to point this out, but this is *not* a horror movie," Nara said, cutting off the nearest undead creature's arm and kicking it backwards. "As long as that spell is still active, we can't just hack these things down and hope they stay dead."

"Then how the hell are we supposed to win?" I asked, running a zombie through. "We don't have infinite energy here, these things will wear us down eventually if they attack like this."

"I have an idea," Nara said. "There's a way Crystal and I can locate the Orb, but it's going to paint a goddamn *massive* target on our heads."

"We'll do what we can," Petra said before any of the rest of us could respond, using two short daggers to deal with two of the creatures at once. "Just...please don't take long, Clint's right, we'll be dead long before they are back in the ground at this rate."

"We need some space so we can form a better defensive line," I said, seeing out of the corner of my eye that Nara and Crystal had gone to the centre of our group. "I don't think these things are going to just stop trying to kill us long enough for us to be able to formulate a real plan."

"Leave that one to me," Marek said. I turned, just in time to spot Marek slamming a fist wreathed in white light into the ground. It caused every zombie and skeleton to collapse to dust. At least temporarily anyway. "Naarin's been training me, he taught me this handy trick in case I needed a bit of breathing space in a fight. I don't think he quite anticipated it making them completely fall apart though."

"That's good enough for now," Petra said. "Ordinarily I wouldn't suggest this, but we can't afford to leave a gap in the circle, for all we know this spell might have more tricks up its sleeve. We'll just have to spread ourselves out and hope we don't regret it."

Just as we were spreading out as evenly as we could, a gurgling sound announced the arrival of more assailants, but now even the skeletons had some semblance of clothing hanging from their body, some of which my inner history nerd recognised as the remnants of World War II military uniform. But even as I swung my blade at a skeleton who got a little too close for comfort, I could feel the air around me changing, the air becoming far colder than I would expect the middle of a desert in bright sunshine would be.

"Nara, Crystal, please tell me that's your doing,"

Mickey called out. "Because this situation is creepy enough without channelling every ghost story I've ever read."

"Well, the good news is we've found the Orb," Nara shouted back. "The bad news…well, I think you'll want to hold onto something…or get airborne double quick."

Niana, stood a short distance to the right of me, shared a confused look with me. "What could you possibly be—" I started saying, but what came next was so sudden I only just had time to mobilise my wings as the sand beneath me suddenly vanished, the only positive being that the collapse was so considerable that some of our assailants were unable to move swiftly enough to get out of the way. Even one zombie with tattered wings was unable to get airborne.

As I turned around to survey the scene, I let out a gasp. Where our defensive perimeter had been stood moments before there was now a large cavern, at the centre of which, in the midst of swirling dark magic that I could see even from my lofty position, Nara and Crystal were struggling to approach a pedestal. On top of the elevated platform was the Orb, which was sending out lashing tendrils of dark magic that Nara and Crystal were barely avoiding.

"We need to distract it," Merzel said. "Maybe we can't dispel it ourselves, but I dread to think what happens if magic capable of raising the dead touches a living creature."

"You know that will mean *we're* in danger, right?" Mickey asked incredulously.

"Maybe," Merzel replied. "But we've got more space to move and more manoeuvrability, I fancy our chances of distracting it long enough for them to finish the job than I do their ability to get close to it without winding up as the living dead themselves."

"Well…this is going to be fun," I said, throwing a spear of ice down at the orb. It dissolved within a matter of inches of it, but the fact that multiple tentacles came flying in our direction at least confirmed that we had the right idea. I found myself and Marek back to back, my heart sinking as I realised that undead fairies had joined the aerial assault. "I don't mean to add any extra pressure," I called out, desperately hoping my friends in the cabin would be able to hear me despite the distance. "But this spell seems to be learning from our tactics, I don't know how long we can keep fighting these things if this keeps up."

"This is probably going to sound crazy," Nara's voice said, coming through telepathically. "But we need you to dive straight down at the Orb."

"Do we get to hear *why* you want us to do this?" I heard Mickey ask.

"Just…trust us," Nara replied. "You'll see what our plan is soon enough. Or die. One of those two."

Part of me felt a rising tide of panic at the end of her sentence, but this was cut short by another zombie fairy aiming its razor-sharp claws at my neck, an attack I just barely managed to move out of the way of. That made my mind up, and as I aimed myself at the centre of the chamber, I could just see out of the corner of my eyes that the others were in similar nose-dives.

But when we were almost close enough that I felt I could have reached out and touched it, there was a sudden burst of bright blue light, and the next thing I knew I was lying against a pillar in one corner of the chamber, the others scattered around, all of them looking as confused as I felt.

"I was trying to use the Orb's own magic against it," Nara said, picking herself up off the floor and then helping Crystal to stand. "But someone teleported it away before I could do so. Someone…it felt like it was Arkelion."

"That's good right?" Merzel said as we all walked over to where Nara and Crystal were stood. "He is a place we know of that these things are completely safe."

I couldn't help noticing that Nara didn't immediately reply, shifting uneasily from foot to foot for a few moments. "You're right," she answered finally. "I suggest we go immediately to China though, if someone *is* controlling these things, then he knows we're fighting back and…I can't imagine he'll not respond in some way."

Rather than returning to check on Selina, as part of me had expected, we instead travelled straight to China, a short distance inside the Chinese side of the Great Wall. The dread hit me almost immediately however, as I realized that where there should have been a flourishing forest, the trees were rotting away…at least, I assumed that that was what was causing the strange creaking noise I could hear around us, until I heard a sudden shout.

"Be careful," Selina called out, surprising all of us as we turned and discovered they were stood next to Petra. Thankfully Selina looked much better than the last time we had seen them. "I got what information from Spyder that I could, but I realized you needed me to join you."

"I appreciate seeing you on your feet," Mickey said, walking over and giving them a hug, which Selina gratefully returned. "But I'm sure we could have managed to deal with this between us."

"I came here because I realized I knew what the spell was," Selina said. "Or, at least, once I'd spoken to Nara's mother I did. Spyder said there were reports going around from tourists walking the Great Wall that the trees in the surrounding area had been moving unnaturally."

"So what?" Merzel asked. "They're either hallucinating or making things up for attention surely?"

"You should pay more attention in your magic lessons Merzel," Selina replied. "There are two spells it sounds like: one is a pretty standard animation spell, which would explain movement to a point but is hardly what a murderous dark magic cult would be interested in frankly. The other is more…worrying. Nara's mother described a spell, without a name that anyone can remember, which doesn't merely animate fauna and inanimate objects, but it corrupts them…bends it to the will of the wielder."

"You're saying this thing corrupts fauna around it?" I asked. "We're stood in the middle of a forest that might be hiding a well of dark magic, and…" I felt my heart sink as I heard a creak, this time much louder and considerably nearer to us. "Oh crap, I had to open my mouth, didn't I?"

I could hear swords being drawn and feel magic being conjured just as we began to see roots being ripped out of the ground three huge trees lumbering towards us, but just as I was about to throw a fireball at the nearest tree, I felt someone grab my arm, and turned to find Niana was trying to prevent me from releasing the spell.

"Clint, we can't attack, something…odd is going on here," she said, pointing at the tree nearest to us, which I realised to my shock wasn't attempting to attack, but was reaching out a branch to us. Even with a lack of translatable language something told me it was the equivalent of a plea for peace. "I've heard myths of ways to communicate with flora…I don't suppose any of us know a way to do that."

"I…I do," Merzel said sheepishly, shifting slightly as he found himself the centre of everyone's attention. "I've always been fascinated by the natural world, my mother taught me a spell which…I'm not sure I'd necessarily describe it as *speaking* to plants, but it allows a version of communing."

"Unless anyone else has a better idea, I think it's our best option," Nara said, offering Merzel a reassuring smile. "They may not be threatening us, but if we make a hostile move towards them that could change *very* quickly. So, maybe we want to lower our weapons right about now?"

There was a moment's pause, followed by the sounds of swords being sheathed and magic dissipating. Merzel stepped towards the closest tree, placing a hand to the bark as green magic formed around him. Nothing seemed to change, but just as I was about to ask a question Merzel turned, his eyes suddenly glowing green.

"Your friend is safe," said Merzel, although his voice was suddenly more ethereal than before. "He is not as familiar with the effects of this magic as he thought, but we wished to communicate with you all directly."

"We?" I asked, feeling a combination of wonder and confusion.

"I've heard of this," Niana replied. "You trees here, you have…I suppose we would call it a hive mind, don't you?"

"That is…not an entirely inaccurate description," 'Merzel' replied. "The magic in this area links every tree and plant you can see, and many you cannot. Ordinarily it protects the inhabitants nearby, but the area has become—"

"Corrupted?" Nara asked. Merzel nodded. "I'm guessing your magic is…containing it for now?"

"You are correct," Merzel answered. "However, the longer the magic is here the less we are able to restrain it, and I fear it will continue to spread if that should happen. Your friend has indicated you wish to help us though."

"We'll do what we can," I said. "But if we are going to do so we need to find the source of this magic, it'll be an Orb, something that would almost certainly look out of place in this area."

There was no vocalised response, instead Merzel lifted his right arm, pointing away from the wall. There, nestled among the trees, was what appeared to be a ruined old temple, but there were two signs that something was not quite right about it: the vines that snaked around it seemed to move unnaturally even as I watched, and there was a similar visible aura of dark magic around it that we had seen before.

"If you guys can get me in there, I can contain the

magic," Nara said. "But you're going to have to keep those vines distracted, which is going to be…fun."

"Well, we've dealt with plenty of horror movie scenarios already," I remarked, only just managing a half-hearted chuckle at the situation we found ourselves in at that moment. "I'll at least take killer vines over zombies any day."

We set off towards the temple, the occasional creaky noise coming from our surroundings but no other overt sign of the trees around us moving. However, as soon as we reached the clearing within, which the temple stood, I had to duck to avoid a whipping vine catching me sharply across the face, which seemed to trigger other flora around us to be drawn in our direction.

"Try avoiding harming them as much as possible," Nara said, Crystal trying to clear a path for her to the entrance to the ruin. "We have to work on the assumption these are only attacking us because they've become corrupted by the magic, if we do too much damage, we could have the whole forest attack us and…in case you haven't noticed, they have us pretty heavily outnumbered here."

"We'll do our best," Mickey said, grunting as he dodged another vine. "It's a pity we don't have a way to tell *them* to ease off on the violence. I never imagined the plant life somewhere would be trying to straight up murder me."

"Well, let's take this as a reminder to always water our houseplants," I said, trying to lighten the mood. "Assuming we're alive long enough to actually get back to said plants."

Although the idea of avoiding harming the plants was honourable on paper, the tendril-like plant appendages were making it difficult to remain even moderately passive.

They seemed to be aiming almost exclusively at our heads, making it especially difficult to try and deflect any incoming assault. I soon found myself cut off from all but Niana and Mickey, although we could hear the occasional shout from the others, with an increasing number of vines drawing in around us.

"Y'know, I used to hate my mum asking me to pull up weeds cos of how hard it was," Mickey said, grunting as he managed to extricate his leg from a plant trying to pull him from his feet. "That seems like a walk in the park compared to fighting these things. I'm not the only person noticing this is getting harder, right?"

"No, I fear you're right," Niana answered him. "The dark magic is getting stronger, but I don't understand how that's even possible, unless—"

Whatever the next part of the sentence was going to be, her words were cut off, a loud bang coming from the direction of the temple, followed by the plants seeming to return to their more passive attitudes and we were reunited with the others. Just as we were sharing a puzzled look Nara stumbled out of the temple, a shaken-looking Crystal leaning against her.

"What happened?" I asked as Petra helped Nara seat Crystal on a fallen tree, the Pixie setting to work ensuring Crystal wasn't hurt. "Was that you two? Arkelion?"

"Neither," Nara said, kissing Crystal's forehead and turning to us. "There was a fairy I've never seen before, I didn't get a proper look at him, but there was one thing that stood out like a sore thumb: he was wearing a ring engraved with the mark of the Drakoni."

"Guys..." Marek said, his voice shaking. "The Orbs... the Cartel...this mystery assailant...Nara's right, isn't she? We've been at the mercy of an unseen enemy all along."

No-one replied for a few moments, I suspected all too stunned to even begin to know what response to give.

"This is a trap," Petra said, finally breaking the silence. "If they're triggering the Orb near Mirallein knowingly, there's every chance they *want* us to go there. There could be an army waiting for us for all we know."

"We don't have a choice," I said, feeling a wave of what I hoped was adrenaline spreading through my veins. "We've seen what these Orbs can do first-hand, if there is even *one* of these weapons in the wrong hands, we can't risk just sitting doing nothing. Admittedly it'd be nice to have some back-up of our own, in case we do run into more than we can handle by ourselves."

"I'll go get Prince Naarin," Marek said. "He may not have an army at his beck and call, but he does have the Royal Guard."

"I thought you hated being left out of the action?" Niana asked, raising an eyebrow.

"Ordinarily yeah," Marek replied, giving us a wry smile. "But if there's an army of dark magicians waiting for us, I'm going to be more use getting us reinforcements than I am joining you in the battle."

"Then go," Nara said, giving him a confident smile. "Tell the Prince to meet us on the coast by the island, if we're not there just assume we've already entered the island and make sure you're well-armed." After Marek had teleported away Nara turned to Selina. "Do you remember the nearest point to Mirallein that you saw the Orb signature?"

"I think so, yes," Selina replied. "Link hands everyone, things might be about to get even uglier."

In a flash we went from an overgrown forest to a sun-drenched clifftop, the first thing I noticed being the island that sat halfway out to sea. Although I'd never been there it made me instantly think of Mont St Michel, except the ruined buildings I could just make out seem to be clinging to jagged cliff faces. However, I could neither see nor feel any magic in the immediate area, dark or otherwise.

"Spread out," Nara said. "There's no way Selina sensed the Orb if it's not here somewhere, but be careful, we don't know what this spell is capable of, I don't want anyone's life in danger because we made a mistake."

We headed off in as many directions as we could, although I realized that Niana and I had ended up holding hands. But as the time passed there wasn't so much as a whiff of magic other than ours, and the loud groan that emanated from Petra was almost impossible to avoid hearing as it seemed to echo all around us.

"So what? Is this Orb some form of invisibility spell?" Petra asked, kicking away a clod of dirt as I turned to look at her. "How the hell do you hide a font of dark magic here? There's barely even a rock to hide the damn thing under."

"Guys, Mirallein is supposed to be empty, right?" Merzel suddenly called out from where we had first materialised. "Because if that's true…we might have a problem."

Petra and I shared a confused look, before we all rushed to where Merzel was. My heart sank as I saw what he meant: dotted among the ruins were fires, fires that I was certain hadn't been there when we arrived. This time none of us felt the need to comment, we all knew what needed to be done. In an instant we were stood at the northern tip of the island, in front of an arch at the top of which had been scrawled the words 'We are Drakon's children'.

"Well, I guess that at least tells us *who* we're dealing with," Mickey said as we stepped through the arch and into the shadowy streets beyond, which snaked upwards between half-collapsed buildings. There was a blast of cold air that rushed past us, causing me to shiver deeply, even as we all spread out, I assumed to cover more ground. "I was expecting a bit much for us to get a welcoming committee, wasn't I?"

"Oh, I wouldn't be so sure of that," came a deep voice from somewhere above us. A figure jumped from a rooftop above us and landing in our centre. It was a fairy, dressed in a long black cloak draped over grey-coloured armour. A mop of grey hair dominated his facial features, one side of which covered an eye, although the other was a strange orange colour. When I looked closer, I realised I could see the same ring Nara had described on his right hand. "We've been waiting for company for so long, you're here to witness a moment of history in the making."

"I don't care what the hell you *think* you're here to do,"

Petra growled. "But you're going to fail, you'll never get your hands on that Orb."

"It's cute that you imagine you can stop us," the fairy said, letting out a guttural laugh. "But I cannot have you interfere." A pulse of purple energy appeared around his hand. "Don't worry, when you wake, you'll have a whole new world to experience, whether you wish it or not."

We all attempted to make a move to prevent him, but even as I moved towards him, he smashed the magic-wreathed hand into the ground, a wave of dark energy spreading out from him. I made a desperate attempt to launch myself into the air, but there was nothing I could do.

"Niana!" I called out in a strangled voice, before the ground rushed up to meet me.

The world went black.

Chapter 17

As she closed her eyes Crystal felt the strangest sensation. She had seen the fairy's magic-wreathed fist crash into the ground, had seen the magic ripple out from him...and yet, rather than it hitting her, it had felt as if she was swimming in the sea and the water was lapping around her. She was almost scared to find out what was happening, but she forced herself to open her eyes and was startled by the sight that confronted her: most of the others were out cold, if seemingly unharmed, leaving only three people still on their feet.

The fairy who had attacked them was looking at her with a mix of surprise and horror, which as she looked down, she realized was due to the fact she was shrouded in dark magic she had unknowingly cast to protect herself, but the bigger surprise was behind the attacker. Mickey was still standing, an amulet clutched tightly in one hand.

"Se...Selina gave it to me," he said, his voice shaking. "I don't think they knew I'd need it for this situation though."

"It worked, that's all that matters," Crystal said, then

spotted something that made her sense of panic return: although the figure was so small it was almost invisible against the surrounding houses, she could just make out a fairy flying up the slope, in the direction of a half-ruined building whose roof was dominated by a beacon that shone with an unnatural green light. "Mickey, that must be where the final Orb is, you *cannot* let them get there first. I'll deal with our…*friend* here."

Mickey paused for a moment, sizing up the enemy in front of him, before nodding, shrinking to fairy size, and flying in the direction of the tower.

"I took out all your friends without breaking a sweat," the other fairy said, laughing. "You *truly* imagine you are capable of even troubling me in a fight? I've studied under the greatest dark magic user this—"

"I get it, you're really good at talking," Crystal said, throwing a bolt of purple lightning at her opponent, a blast that the fairy just barely dodged out of the way of, his cloak being singed. "But rather than *telling* me how good you are, why don't you *show* me."

"Oh, I'm going to enjoy killing your friends when I'm done with you," the fairy replied, raising one hand as vines started to grow up around Crystal, who used a mixture of fire spells and her sword to break free of them. "I forgot to introduce myself, I do have some code of honour. My name is Ithire Drakon, leader of the Children of Drakon," Ithire dove straight at Crystal, who was forced to shrink to avoid him colliding with her.

"I don't care if you're the damn king of Ireland," Crystal replied, conjuring a bolt of ice that grazed Ithire's cheek, feeling a small dose of satisfaction that it drew blood. "These things have killed hundreds already, nobody can actually be naïve enough to think they can control magic that powerful?"

"I don't need to control them," Ithire replied, laughing as shadows began to rise from the ground, grabbing onto Crystal's leg. "You silly little children *still* have no concept what is happening here, do you?" He pulled his hand towards his body, the shadows drawing Crystal closer. "He's made it child's play to figure out his plan and you're too thick to pay any attention to the signs."

"I'm not sure that *I'm* the one who needs to be more observant," Crystal said, letting out a laugh as she released a fireball at almost point-blank range, breaking the spell and allowing her to fly backwards and producing a wave of ice that collided midway between them with Ithire's wave of green magic. "We have a saying where I come from, 'all mouth, no trousers', I'm beginning to wonder if the person who came up with that had been watching you trying to wield magic."

"You have a good grasp of dark magic," came Ithire's voice, although Crystal suddenly realised she could no longer see him anywhere. "But I have had a lifetime to learn how to control power like this." By the time she realised that the voice was coming from directly behind her it was too late. Rather than using the shadows to pull her towards him, the dark fairy used them to throw her across the courtyard, causing her to land hard on her right arm with an audible yelp. "There are so many uses for dark magic," he said, warping so that he was stood with a boot on her stomach.

"Maybe I'll give your little girlfriend a personal demonstration once I'm through killing you."

"If you touch a hair on her head," Crystal growled, her eyes beginning to turn dark red, "I will make your death feel like an eternity."

But, just as her magic was forming around her right hand there was a whistling noise, an arrow burying itself in Ithire's shoulder, which seemed to shock him enough to prevent the killing blow. Even as he attempted to recover a second arrow struck him in the centre of the chest, leaving him stumbling backwards.

"Hey, asshole," Crystal shouted, a knife formed of purple light gripped in one hand. "Say hello to my dad when you see him." She threw it, the blade burying itself in his heart before he could even respond, his head lolling backwards as he collapsed forward. Crystal's eyes returned to their normal green colour, as she turned to find Nikkela marching towards her, her bow in one hand. Two fairies in the garb of the Royal Guard followed close behind her, their swords sheathed but kept close to hand.

"Find the Prince, tell him his sister and the others are safe," Nikkela said, walking over to help Crystal to her feet once the guards had vanished. "The love of my life thought you might need some medical aid, and while I may not be a full-time warrior like him that doesn't mean I've forgotten how to use this bow." She took a look around the rest of the group's unconscious forms. "Are they hurt in any way?"

"I can't say I had much chance to stop and check," Crystal replied, letting out a wry chuckle. "I'm hoping the fact that we're not surrounded by pools of blood is a good thing though."

"I'm going to point this out before someone else does though," Nikkela said, leaning down to rest her hand on Niana's arm to begin the healing process. "Where's Mickey? He definitely came with you, but I don't see him here."

Crystal was in such shock at her dark powers being unleashed that she didn't initially pick up on Nikkela's question, finally breaking from her trance when Nara knelt down in front of her, her memory of the events prior to the battle flooding back to her.

"The tower," Crystal said. "There was another enemy, I saw him fly towards the tower and told Mickey to…If he's as powerful as the one I just fought Mickey could be in serious danger."

"Nikkela, find my brother," Niana said, turning to the healer. "He needs to evacuate the island *now*." She couldn't help a sigh at the incredulous look the other fairy gave her. "I don't have time to explain, these weapons have shown themselves capable of killing hundreds at the drop of a hat, I won't have my brother staying in the danger zone because he decided to be a hero."

"I'll try my best," Nikkela said. "Just be aware that I may be his soulmate, that doesn't give me the ability to stop him if decides to come help though. You guys need to focus on that tower, leave the rest to me."

Through a combination of running, flying and teleporting we soon found ourselves at the tower's entrance. There was a large oak door whose lintel was covered in images of wolves and a strange language that seemed reminiscent of a combination of Italian and fairy tongues I had read: but I could make no sense of it. As soon as she was certain we were all there Petra shoulder-charged the door, which offered her no resistance. The tower's ground floor was one large room, above which hung the rotting remains of what I could only assume had been the rest of the tower at one time. But it only took a few moments for my eye to be drawn to the most important aspect of the room: At the far end Mickey was stood, his arm pinning a ragged looking older male fairy to the wall, a knife in one hand. As we got nearer, I noticed he too was wearing a Drakonite ring.

"No offence Mickey, but let me take over," Petra said, putting a hand on his shoulder. "I'm not calling you soft, but I'm a little more prepared to be…rough when the situation requires it." Mickey let the fairy go, but Petra pinned him in place with her magic before he had any chance to flee. "We can do this the nice way, or this can hurt *a lot*. So before you decide to keep your trap shut I suggest you consider your options *very carefully*."

The trapped fairy let out a guttural laugh. "You think I'm going to resist? We *wanted* you here. My name is Saviran, you played right into our plan."

"Let me guess," Mickey said, letting out a loud sigh. "The last Orb is supposed to be triggered when we're all in one spot? I can't help wondering why we can't so much as sense anything in the area though."

"You're looking for a weapon?" Saviran asked. "The last Orb isn't a weapon, it was designed to help those who asked it to locate the greatest stock of dark magic relics on the surface of this pitiful world." He snapped his fingers, the light above us suddenly changing. I looked up, finding that not only had an Orb materialised halfway between us and what was left of the ceiling of the structure, but it seemed to be projecting the image of a map into the air around us. This eventually focused into what could have been mistaken for a photo of a large mountain range, in the background of which was a tall, slender tower we all recognised immediately.

"The Ravenspire…" I uttered under my breath, feeling my blood run cold.

"Guys, I know where that is," Mickey said, his voice shaking. "My only ever skiing holiday was in that area, it's in the French Alps. Who managed to hide *that* in the middle of a skiing area?"

"I don't know, but I'd take a bet all of this is linked," Petra said angrily, turning around to speak to Saviran, only to realise his body was wasting away in front of their eyes. "Damnit, how did I not know he'd pull that stunt?"

I moved towards him, only to have my progress blocked by Petra. "I might be able to save him, we could ask him more questions."

"I appreciate the enthusiasm, but that won't work," Petra said, grimacing as the last glimmer of life faded from Saviran. "What he just did…it's the magical equivalent of having a cyanide pill lodged in his tooth, once he triggered it no amount of healing magic would've been capable of reversing it." She looked at the image of the Ravenspire hovering above us. "So, this is both the one place we need to go, and the last place on the planet we should probably be. There's no way Drakoni fanboys have a map to the place and it *isn't* a trap."

"That's why you need to go," came a male voice from behind us, quickly revealed to be Prince Naarin as he stepped into the centre of the room. "If even half the stories of that place are true, what do you imagine will happen if it falls into the hands of a more dangerous group? The Children of Drakon won't be the only creatures interested in access to forbidden relics."

"Is this where you're insisting you come with us?" Niana asked, taking my hand in hers. "Getting bored of not getting to go off on adventures?"

"Not at all," Naarin replied, chuckling for a moment before he became deadly serious once again. "I suggest you only take the group you already have." He walked over to Niana, handing his sister a necklace on the end of which was a golden pegasus. "If you do run into trouble, Niana knows how to use this, I'll sense it wherever I am and be with you as soon as possible." He walked back towards the doorway, stopping briefly to look back at us. "Good luck, I fear we may all need it."

It took us two leaps, since none of us had been close to the Spire itself before, but we finally arrived at a village on the slopes beneath our destination. At least, it must have been a village at some point, but judging by the crumbling ruins that surrounded us it hadn't been occupied for quite some time. We moved through it in silence, Niana cuddling closer to me as a bitingly cold wind blasted through our group. As we finally reached the Ravenspire itself I couldn't help looking up at the structure. It stretched so far above us that I couldn't tell if clouds were obscuring the top of the tower or not. Directly in front of us however was a pair of iron doors, around which were inscribed strange images and words, some in languages I could understand.

"It's all some variation of Raven, or Crow, or...other names I don't recognise," Selina said, taking a step towards the door. "Geez, whoever built this place was a little bit on the nose with the decoration, weren't they?" They reached out to touch the doors, before withdrawing their hand suddenly. "I was ready to blast this door down if that was what was required, but...the door is unlocked. Someone's expecting us, and I don't know whether that's more or *less* terrifying."

"Let's get in before our host changes their mind," Petra said, pushing the door open confidently, the rest of us hurrying in after her. "Well...I don't know whether this is what I expected or a disappointment."

My eyes slowly adjusted to how little the room was illuminated compared to outside, the ground floor's sole window providing barely any more light than was being produced by a pair of lanterns hanging on the walls. We were stood inside a circular room, at the far end of which was a stone staircase that seemed to loop around a central pillar, both set into a floor formed of slate grey stones. Against another wall was a large wooden bookcase, filled with books and scrolls, and even a strange golden spherical object that rested on top of a small plinth.

"In fairness Petra they're not just going to leave a load of dark magic artefacts on the ground floor where just anyone can pick them up," Selina said, walking over to the bookcase and studying it closely. "We need to make a plan though, this place is huge, we have no idea where to even *start* looking, we could be here for hours and not have come *close* to finding what we need."

The debate raged on, but I lost track, finding my mind drawn to another voice that seemed to whisper around the room. All I was certain of was that it wasn't one of my friends, and the more I tried to concentrate on it, the more I realised there were multiple voices speaking, although I could only make out a single male voice clearly:

"*The Spire knows all…*" the voice almost sang more than spoke. "*The answers await you…just take the stairs…your eyes will be opened.*"

Before I knew it, and with no idea why I was doing so, I was walking towards the stairs. I felt as if I was in a trance, feeling a suspicion something was wrong but unable to persuade my body to stop, never mind turn around. The effect only broke when I reached the third step, a loud crack sounding as my foot landed on the step. I turned around, just in time to see the air shimmer as a bubble formed, cutting me off from the others and also cutting them off from the door we had entered through. I immediately drew my sword, moving towards the bubble, but Niana took a step towards me.

"Clint, darling, you know I love your bravery," she said, her voice sounding strangely echoed through the barrier.

"But we don't know what magic created this, attacking it could have any number of effects."

"I'm not leaving you trapped here," I said, looking around the perimeter in a vain attempt to spot some kind of weakness to exploit. "If something happened to you—"

"Clint, look at me," Niana said, reaching out to touch the barrier, a gesture I copied. "We're as safe here as we would be outside with you, but right now we have bigger things to worry about. Whatever is behind all this...whoever caused this...should be in this tower. You need to go find them." For a few moments I considered arguing, but I knew deep down she was right, so nodded. We both rested our foreheads against the barrier, in a vain attempt to feel close to each other. "I know I say it a lot, but I love you."

"I love you too," I replied, lingering for a moment before pulling away again. "I promise I'll be back for you as soon as I can." With one last lingering look I shrunk myself, flying upwards and leaving the others behind.

None of the trapped group had any idea how long they'd been sat there, whether it was 5 minutes or fifty, when the sound of Marek throwing a small rock against the barrier finally made Selina snap.

"Marek, that is *not* helping," Selina growled, almost immediately regretting it when they saw the frightened look he gave her. "I'm sorry, I'm suddenly beginning to understand the concept of cabin fever. I'm almost missing people trying to kill us." She turned to where Nara and Petra were stood, deep in conversation, next to the bookcase. "I don't suppose either of you are any closer to finding a way out of this?"

"I'm afraid not," Petra replied. "We can't teleport, the barrier appears impenetrable...I'm starting to fear the only way of lowering this barrier is outside of our reach. Unless Niana's locket is showing any sign of achieving anything?"

"Not unless any of you know a way to work this that I'm not aware of," Niana said, sighing as she returned the necklace to the pocket of her dress. "We're running out of options here, we need to consider our next move if we can't get out of here." Just as the others were moving towards her, they all heard a new sound: a pair of heavy footsteps descending the stairs. "That...that doesn't sound like Clint," Niana said, Petra taking a step towards the stairs as the footsteps came closer. Finally, the newcomer revealed themselves.

Arkelion, dressed in a far more elaborate robe than he had worn before, a silver necklace around his neck. Petra and Merzel seemed relieved at their mentor's appearance, but Nara's hand shot almost immediately to her blade, although she didn't draw it immediately.

"Master Arkelion, thank goodness, you can free us," Merzel said, stepping towards him. "We need to find our way to the top of the tower."

"Oh, my sweet, naïve friend, I'm afraid I will *not* be doing that," Arkelion said, letting out a low laugh as he reached out, the shield opening in front of him as if it was nothing more than a screen door, only for it to close again behind him once he had stepped inside. "My young associates and I must have a conversation, so I cannot have any of you interrupting me." He reached out his hand, which glowed dark purple as all but Merzel and Petra found themselves pinned to the wall, their mouths sealed with a strange black substance, a sob escaping Merzel as the twins took in the scene around them, before Petra whirled round to face the older fairy.

"What the *hell* did you just do?" she shouted. "Let our friends go, they've been helping us, they've been helping *you*."

"Of course they have," Arkelion replied, laughing. "You all have, more than any of you have begun to realise. Although, to be fair to that Pixie scum," he said, spitting on the floor near where Nara hung, trying fruitlessly to struggle against her bonds, "she and your friend Clint have begun to suspect I'm not who I appear to be, it's why we had to bring our original plan forward somewhat."

"Don't talk to her like that," Merzel said, his hands balling into fists. "Why would you be rude to our own people."

"She is no more *your* people than *you* are mine," Arkelion snapped at him, his eyes turning white. "To think I ever thought you your sister's equal, you are a weak little coward who *wishes* he knew what magic was. Petra..." He paused, turning to face her as a wicked smile crossed his face. "You have so much potential, more than you've begun to realise."

"You say we don't know who you really are," Petra said, placing herself between her brother and Arkelion. "You better start explaining, *now*. Is Arkelion even your real name?"

"There was an Arkelion once, centuries ago, but you're right, that is not my real name," the older fairy said, rolling the right sleeve of his cloak up, revealing the gold bracelet on his wrist. He placed his left hand on it, muttering something under his breath that caused the bracelet to glow, before removing it to reveal a logo which made Petra's blood run cold. "My name, my *real* name, is Geth'ra, I was one of the Drakonite inner circle back in the old days."

"That's…that's not possible," Petra said, feeling the courage drain from her. "The Cult were slaughtered to a man centuries ago, you *cannot* be here."

"You have such a basic knowledge of magic my dear," Geth'ra said, not even attempting to hide his amusement. "Life can be extended far beyond its natural limits with the right…*assistance*. Besides, as you said, they believed my kin dead after the Battle of Mirallein, why would they come looking for someone who knew how to hide themselves in plain sight." He smiled broadly, revealing teeth that suddenly seemed unnaturally sharp. "You and your idiot friends actually thought you were preventing evil, you were doing *exactly* what we wanted all along."

"What do you want with us?" Petra asked, trying to steady herself. "What could you *possibly* imagine you can offer me that I would even *begin* to entertain?"

"I told you already Petra, you have a unique power set among inhabitants of your city," Geth'ra replied. "It is why I was so keen to take you under my wings. You have come so far in your short life but…you are capable of so much more. I could give you your wildest dreams, this world would bow before you once you have learnt how to wield the spells I know."

Petra paused, for a moment considering the offer, before her expression became grim, and she fixed her gaze on Geth'ra. "You know nothing about me, because if you did, you'd realise I would *die* before I accepted the power you allowed to corrupt you. There is nothing you could offer me that I'd accept."

"*Foolish girl,*" Geth'ra growled, clenching his fist and using his magic to slam Petra into the ground, winding her instantly. "Your pitiful little group has already lost, I am offering you a way to save yourself." He stepped towards her, drawing his sword and pointing it at her neck. "You're just the same as your parents, just as weak as they always were."

"You know nothing about our parents," Petra gasped. "They would *never* befriend a monster like you."

"I knew them better than either of you did," Geth'ra said, laughing. "They called me friend once, but they would never have allowed me to train you, they were too... squeamish about your potential. And so, they had to be removed, permanently."

"You...you..." Petra stammered. "You killed them..."

"Did you never wonder why I knew where their bodies were?" Geth'ra asked. "Your people were so wracked with grief and concern for you two they never thought to ask any questions. It doesn't matter though," he said, raising his sword over his head. "You'll see them again soon enough."

"Get away from her," came a sudden, loud voice, the

room being filled with a bright light as a pulse of white magic threw Geth'ra against the pillar, pinning him to it. Petra looked around, stunned to discover the source was Merzel. Her brother was wreathed in white light, his eyes the same colour, a look of grim determination on his face.

"How…how is this possible?" Geth'ra asked. "You're a runt, you're—"

"Weak?" Merzel asked, clenching his fists. "All I ever wanted was to gain your approval. All I *wanted* was a father figure, and not only did you treat me like worse than nothing, you *killed* the only father I will ever have." Petra realised to her surprise that tears were in Merzel's eyes as he spoke. "When you stopped teaching me, I locked myself in the library and taught myself. It turns out I had plenty of potential, just not the kind *you* wanted."

"You won't kill me," Geth'ra said, smirking. "I don't care how much power you've learnt, you're still a coward, you'll fail just like you always do."

"He might not have it in him to kill you," Petra said, struggling to her feet, her breath still ragged, as she started walking gingerly towards him. "You…you never knew me. My mother taught me to hate dark magic, my father taught me to stand up to bullies…you and your magic represent everything I would wipe from this world if I could." She picked up Geth'ra's own blade, stepping closer.

"You'll never be what you deserve," Geth'ra spat. "You are giving up the chance to rule this world as fairies *deserve* to."

"I've seen what your version of *ruling* means," Petra said, not even flinching as she stood in front of him. "All *you* deserve is justice. For Glasswater, for all the fairies you and your kin have caused the deaths of. But most of all...*this*," she uttered, bringing the sword round in an arc and beheading Geth'ra is one stroke, "is for my mother." As his headless body dropped to the floor it was like all the adrenaline drained from her body in one go, and Petra fell to her knees, letting the sword fall down next to her as the others were released from their bindings. "I'm...Merzel, I'm so sorry, if I'd known what he—"

"Petra, you don't need to apologise," Merzel said, walking over to her looking back to his normal self, resting a hand on her shoulder. "He lied to both of us, I know you would've protected me if you'd known." He drew her into a hug, both of them shaking slightly. "He's gone now, he can't harm any of us."

"It's not just you he tricked," Nara said, the shield that had trapped them disintegrating around them. "We have to assume everything he told us was a lie. Which means that the most dangerous magical artefacts this world has ever known could be anywhere now, and we have no idea—"

Her sentence was cut short by a sudden scream from Niana, and they turned to find her clutching her head, her eyes closed.

"There's...there's someone else here," she stuttered out.

"We know about Clint," Mickey said, the laugh he had begun dying on his lips as he saw how pale Niana had turned. "Niana, who are you talking about?"

"The top of the tower," she said, sobbing. "There is something impossibly ancient, and far more powerful than *anything* I have sensed, even Feth'rael, waiting at the top of this tower."

They all turned towards the stairs Clint had ascended as Niana spoke again.

"And Clint is heading straight for them."

Chapter 18

I found myself climbing the tower by alternating between flying and walking. The staircase was too narrow to fly all the way up in one go, but there were far too many stairs for even the durable person to climb with no break. Occasionally there was a landing, 'Only one door led from each of the occasional landings. Most were shut, something in the pit of my stomach telling me it was a bad idea to open them. But three were open. One contained weapons, from small hunting knives to a large, razor sharp pike. Another was stacked with scrolls so covered in dust I could only begin to imagine how long they had laid there. The third was full of books, one of whose front cover was turned towards me; I had the niggling feeling I recognised the golden design from somewhere, but at that point my mind was drawing a complete blank. Finally, after what seemed an eternity, I reached the top of the tower, finding myself in front of an incredibly weathered oak door. The door otherwise was unremarkable, but the same crows and ravens that surrounded the entrance to the Spire covered the lintel. Just as I reached out to touch the handle the door suddenly swung inward, and I found myself unable to resist the urge to step inside.

Most of the room was so dark that I struggled to estimate its size, the only illumination available coming from a large window to my left, a pair of heavy shutters just visible opened wide.

"Ah, Clint, I have been looking forward to this greatly," came a voice from the darkness, my hand moving to my sword immediately. "Oh, come now, if you and your friends were capable of being *any* kind of threat with your weak excuse for magic, what makes you believe I would allow you to enter this place to begin with?"

I felt a chill run down my spine, as I realized I could sense the dark magic in the room. I moved my hand away from my sword.

"Who are you?" I asked, trying, and failing, to locate the source of the voice. "No-one I've heard of has come across a fairy called the Lord of Ravens, most people barely know *this* place exists."

"Have you not considered I *wanted* it this way?" the voiced asked, a deep laugh echoing around the room. "Besides, you have made a great error, I am no fairy, but I should start from the beginning. You should be familiar with my friends, if not me." A golden image formed in front of me, that for a few moments I didn't recognise, but as it became clear the colour drained from my face. The image was unmistakable.

The same image I had seen in the fortress of the Cartel.

The same image I had seen on the book further down the tower.

The mark of the Drakoni.

"You *can't* be one of the Drakoni," I said, struggling to comprehend what was playing out in front of me. "That would make you centuries old, *no* magic is capable of that."

"You think because you can heal your friends you know *anything* about how magic truly works?" the voice spat back. "You have barely scratched the surface of what magic is capable of, but I have many secrets to share with you."

There was the sound of a wooden board creaking, and the source of the voice finally revealed itself: It was a man, well over six foot tall, draped in a long cloak that appeared to be formed of raven feathers, although I couldn't believe something that intricate could be created from those. His face was grey and covered in wrinkles, a pair of intense black eyes staring back at me from beneath tousled grey hair. I couldn't help a shocked gasp escaping my mouth.

"What? Were you expecting a fairy?" the figure asked, letting out a deep chuckle.

"Humans...humans can't...can't use magic," I stuttered. "And I was told you died before the end of the Battle of Mirralein."

"You don't even know my name, do you?" the figure asked, stepping closer, dark magic radiating off him. "My name is Elaric. Or, at least, it was. I much prefer my title as Lord of Ravens. As for how I survived, do humans not have a saying that goes 'History is written by the victors'? If my death was reported by the brave alliance of 'light' that felled my cult, no-one would go looking for me. Especially when they believed their fae bogeyman was the real threat in the Cult."

"You let them see what you wanted them to," I said under my breath. "But how…how did you escape Mirralein and get here without *someone* seeing you?"

"The minion who would become your 'friend' Arkelion," Elaric replied, my mind immediately leaping to my friends below, but I found myself unable to move. "He…*convinced* some of the victorious soldiers to dispose of the Orbs, their leaders were too busy worrying about their fate to come looking for a man they believed dead. I tracked their delivery of our relics here, and set to work studying the tower's contents, while using the occupants of the city below to sustain my life. Admittedly I would almost certainly have died centuries ago if not for *his* help."

"What do you mean…his…" I froze, for the first time sensing something I hadn't picked up on before. There was only Elaric and I in the room and yet…I could sense a third presence. One emanating from where Elaric was stood. "What…what *are* you?"

"You see, my kind go by many names Clint," Elaric replied, a purple tinge suddenly visible faintly in his eyes. "The Unseen, the Overlords…there is even a world that foolishly calls us the Creators…if only they knew the truth of us." He let out a sinister laugh. "Although, you will likely know us as the Timeless."

The memory came to me in an instant. "The Mirror, the voice I heard…that was you, wasn't it?"

"Not me I'm afraid," Elaric replied. "But yes, my kind corrupted the Timeless Oak lifetimes ago, those fool guardians around it were too blind to realise they were protecting the very evil they fought to keep out."

"Why?" I asked, trying to move my arm to cast a spell but finding myself suddenly transfixed. "The Orbs, the teenagers, Arkelion…what was the purpose of all this, and why not aid Feth'rael?"

"Feth'rael was a fool of a 'god'," Elaric replied, spitting as he spoke the name. "He fought the enemy he *wanted* you to be, rather than teaching you a lesson in *real* power. But now…now his mistake has made magic so much stronger, both light and dark. And that's before we consider that *you* gave me the weapons I need."

"But we gave them…to…" I closed my eyes. The minute he mentioned Arkelion I should have realised. "What have we done?"

"You've given us *everything* I could have wanted," Elaric replied, an unpleasant smirk on his face. "I am going to show humans that magic is not merely the toy of the fae race, I am going to show this world what *real* darkness means."

"I would die before I'd let you harm this world," I managed to snarl at him. "Before I let you harm my *friends*."

"It's almost sweet you imagine you can prevent this," Elaric laughed. "You are so many steps behind me: your friends just freed me and they don't even *know* about that. But I promise you, this is not personal," he said, bending down so that his unnatural looking eyes were level with mine. "Oh Clint, you, your friends…your world…you are about to be part of something *so much bigger* than you comprehend. It will make what I'm about to do look like child's play in comparison." He stood up straight, springing surprisingly quickly onto the window. "I'm afraid I cannot waste any more time on our discussion Clint," he said, with a snap of his fingers suddenly turning him into a raven, which fixed its eyes on me. "But we will meet again, *that* is a promise."

With that, and before I could make any kind of response, the bird launched from the windowsill, vanishing into the sky. I collapsed to my knees, too shocked to do anything but stare at the spot where Elaric had been stood a moment before. I was so dumbstruck I didn't realise the others had reached the room till Niana pulled me into a hug, rubbing a hand up and down my back.

"Clint, you're freezing," she said, letting go of me enough to look straight into my eyes. "What in the *world* happened up here?"

"We…we made a mistake," I finally managed to say. "We gave him exactly what he wanted."

"We know about Arkelion," Petra replied, coming round to face me. "He's dead, it should be easy to find the Orbs—"

"He was only a puppet," I replied. "Elaric…the human who led the Drakoni…Petra, not even Feth'rael was as strong as what I sensed him to be. He was using the Orbs…the secrets of this place…"

"We beat Feth'rael," Marek said confidently. "We've beaten every challenge we faced before, what's an aging fairy going to do to us that a literal *god* couldn't?"

"He's no mere fairy," Niana said, shaking so much I felt the need to pull her close to me. "Marek, Clint…everyone…if what I sensed was correct, I don't know how we defeat him. I'm not sure we even *can*."

"The world is heading for a disaster," I said, looking out of the window, feeling tears forming in my eyes.

"And it's all our fault."

To Be Continued...

Epilogue

Tom Daniels was frustrated. He had only been back from college five minutes and *already* his mother was sending him to find his brother Jake, who was about ten minutes from missing his curfew. Tom walked into the front garden, spotting Jake's favourite ball on the grass but still no sign of his sibling.

"Okay Jake, I get it, you like acting like a brat when I'm home," Tom called out, heading for the sidewalk. "If you don't get here now, I'll make sure you don't get more ice cream until…" He trailed off, having finally located Jake. About 30 yards up the road Jake was leaning against his bike talking to a figure that, although he couldn't make out any features other than dark clothing and blue hair, immediately put him on guard. "Jake, get away from him," he called out. "You *know* what mum says about talking to strangers."

"Do listen to your brother Jacob," the figure growled, causing Jake to drop his bike and run screaming towards the house. "Besides, it's your brother I'm *truly* looking for." Before Tom could try to run himself, the figure suddenly appeared in front of him, revealed to be a fairy with unkempt grey hair, pale skin and red eyes, who wrapped a hand around Tom's throat. "It's been so long since I've had a proper feed," he said, reaching a hand out as his victim's body became encased in ice, spreading down from his chest.

"You *could* do that Malaire," came a voice from behind him, "but I'm sure one of Feth'rael's own generals is capable of better than that."

"Keep that scum's name away from me," Malaire said, not turning to look at the voice's source. "He *left* me like this, I deserve to feed in peace."

"What if I told you I could free you of this...hunger forever?" the voice asked. "That I could free you of this curse?"

"No-one can promise *that*," Malaire replied, finally turning to find Elaric stood behind him, now looking closer to a healthy human, although his eyes were still black. "A *human* seeks to tell me what I can and can't do with my power?" Malaire asked, laughing loudly. "Go now and *maybe* I won't feed on you next."

"I am no mere human," Elaric said, raising his hand. "I am this world's future, but you..." He paused clenching his hand as a cloud of what seemed like black mist was torn from Tom, his lifeless body collapsing to the floor as the mist formed a ball of energy hovering in front of Elaric. "You may call me by my new name, the Raven God. There is more power where this came from, if you are willing to join me."

Malaire looked between his own body, Tom's remains, and Elaric, only needing a moment to decide. He reached out, the energy leaping to him and surrounding his body. When it finally cleared, he had changed. He looked almost like any other fairy, but taller, more muscled, and with dark magic visible swirling under his skin.

"This…this is glorious," Malaire said, laughing as he turned to look at the razor-sharp wings that emerged from his back, before finally turning to Elaric once again. "So, what is it we are going to do with all this power?"

"Oh, now the real fun begins," Elaric replied, a wide grin spreading across his face. "The Dark Leylines have remained hidden long enough. It's time to show this world what it is *truly* made of."

Acknowledgements

To Craig for being willing to take on another book after Fairy War, Alison for doing a great job editing and for putting up with a few panicked conversations when I was struggling, Francisco for another great proofreading job.

To my friends and family for putting up with yet another round of excited and worried discussions about the story while always being supportive, and Dad for the usual rounds of editing before it reached Craig.

Last, but by no means least, RJ Anderson, whose fairy novels inspired me to take my first steps into the Fae Age and beyond.

About the Author

E.J. is an avid gamer, reader and comic book movie fan, who belongs to more fandoms than can be counted. When they're not geeking out over the newest Marvel movie they can be found writing one of her many stories, of which the Fae Age is only a single corner of.

https://twitter.com/thefaeage

Also from Deep Hearts YA

The Reign of Ruth
Jazel L. Faith

In the Forest of Dahlia's depths, witches have long hidden from the clutches of malicious hunters. But as their numbers dwindle and hope fades, they turn to a sacrifice to create the most formidable witch to ever exist: Ruby, known only as the Red Demon.

Bound by fate, Ruby is thrust into a treacherous quest for freedom, her only ally being Lilith, a witch with the power to glimpse into the future. Together, they venture beyond their sanctuary, stepping into a world of hunters, life-changing discoveries, secrets, royalties, and magic to seek peace for their kind at last.

The girls will soon learn that no battle comes without sacrifice, and their choices hold the power to shape the destinies of all witches.

Available now in ebook and paperback

Also from Deep Hearts YA

Mark of Ravage and Ruin
Jacyn Gormish

When Barli wakes up in a religious-run prison called the Asylum, she has one goal: get out and back to her girlfriend.

The Priest that runs the Asylum sees something more in Barli. He sees an assassin in the making. He pushes her into training to become a Black Sin, a killer for the clergy, free to roam the streets and eliminate anyone he wants removed from society.

For Barli, this is a way to escape and get back to her girlfriend's arms. She plays along with the Priest's plans, even if she has no desire to be a Black Sin.

But the friendships she develops along the way take her by surprise. In particular, she becomes fond of Ferran, a boy locked in the asylum for life for reasons she doesn't know...if there is even a valid reason for the power-hungry Priest to do such a thing.

When Barli's opportunity finally arises to set out into the city and escape to her lover, she learns something that stops her in her tracks.

Ferran is to be killed.

And only Barli can save him.

Available now in ebook and paperback

www.ingramcontent.com/pod-product-compliance
Lightning Source LLC
Chambersburg PA
CBHW051129020726
47501CB00005B/1426